ALL WORK, NO PLAY

ASSA RAYMOND BAKER

Good2Go Publishing

ALL WORK NO PLAY

Written by Assa Ray Baker

Cover Design: Davida Baldwin

Typesetter: Mychea

ISBN: 9781947340190

Copyright © 2018 Good2Go Publishing

Published 2018 by Good2Go Publishing

7311 W. Glass Lane • Laveen, AZ 85339

www.good2gopublishing.com

https://twitter.com/good2gobooks

G2G@good2gopublishing.com

www.facebook.com/good2gopublishing

www.instagram.com/good2gopublishing

ACKNOWLEDGMENTS

All praise be to God, Lord of my world! Nobody told me that the sky was the limit. So I grew up with a fear of heights, like every one of the men that became my brothers in the streets. I'm not gonna name all of you, just the ones that started from the bottom with me and have always had my back: J. McNutt a.k.a. Flex, M. Danley a.k.a. Moe, D. Ashford a.k.a. Dee, them Cunningham brothers—RIP—Tim and Alfonica "Junior" Jones, J. Ross a.k.a. Daddy O., and D. Wayett a.k.a. Damoe. Like I said, I'm not going to name all of you, and if you know me then you know it's all love with us. I send my love and prayers to my beautiful children and the women who made them. I need to say thank you to my dad for stepping up as much as he could for me in my time of need—RIP, Jim Ray Jones III. I miss you much. I just have to put this name in here because she's crazy and I don't want to hear it LOL: Orean Harper a.k.a. Chocolate, and family. Look, I'll have more room to add everyone else in my next one, because I'm not done yet. Thank You to G2G for taking me in and bringing my dream to life.

ALL WORK,
NO PLAY

PROLOGUE

After Chicago drug kingpin J. Ross is released from jail, he vows vengeance on the ones who he believes put him there. So he sends Vudu, a vicious hit man who is sworn to carry out the contract on their heads, to Milwaukee.

Kadeem and Gully play the game the way it's supposed to be played. One is a brilliant rapper hustling to fund his dream of making it big while the other uses the game as a means to give his growing family the life he was not privileged to grow up in on the ghetto streets.

GP, a part-time student, and her step-brother, Calboy, play the other side of the game. Larceny is their main hustle. But their crew only hits those who are in the game, and they never bend that rule.

On one side is greed, and the other is envy. Once the two are placed into the equation, friendship and loyalty go up in smoke fast. And with murder in everyone's eyes, it becomes hard to focus on their dreams as the streets of Milwaukee get even more deadly.

All Work, No Play is a nicely-paced, exciting urban thriller filled with drama, sex, and murder that promises to take you on an exciting tour through the streets without you getting out of your seat.

<u>ONE</u>

GP

It was just after 6:00 a.m. when we re-entered the afterset held on 34th and Clerk. By this time, most of its crowd had gone, leaving behind a few of the ghetto's ballas and hard-core gamblers. They were all too self-indulged in games of dice, drinking, drugging, and gold-digging to take notice of the three of us taking our positions and masking our faces with the half masks that we wore around our necks.

"It's party time for real now! Nobody move, and nobody gets shot today!" Calboy yelled once he saw we were ready.

"On second thought, just lay the fuck down so I won't have to hurt one or two of you muthafuckas!"

I spotted my help standing next to who she had planned on peeling for a buck or two after giving him the time of his of life.

"Not you in the black dress! Here! Take this bag and pick up every cent in this room. Bitch, if ya think it'll make me a dollar, put it in the bag!"

I tossed her the knapsack off my shoulder.

"Y'all don't make it hard on her. Empty your pockets! Give it all up!" Lyte ordered from her position next to the well-stocked makeshift bar.

She calmly swept the room while showing off her fully loaded extended-clip MAC-10.

A cubby man emerged from a doorway to the right of me. "Oh shit!"

"What the fuck!" he howled as he tried to free his gun from his belt to be a hero.

But all the partying and drugging made him a few seconds too slow.

"Don't do it! Drop it!" I warned from behind him.

"Bitch-ass nigga! She told ya to drop it!" Calboy yelled.

Calboy then hit him in the face with the butt of the big Hi-Point 45 while simultaneously peeling the gun from the now bloodied man's fingers.

"Thanks! Now since you up, you can take me to the money."

Calboy remembered cubby as one of the guys throwing the afterset when they had stalked the place earlier.

"Okay! Okay! Just don't kill me," the cubby pled as he did what he was told.

He then escorted Calboy back into the room that he had

come out of, this time leaving a trail of blood as he went.

A distinguished-looking man in his early fifties or late forties raised his hand like a schoolboy.

"What, Pops?" I said as I turned my Glock on him.

"Ms. Lady, you don't gotta point that at me. I won't try you."

He had seen that my gun didn't move.

"Do you know who this set belongs to?"

I didn't answer.

"It's mine. I'm Papa Luv. If y'all just stop and go out the way ya came, I'll let y'all breathe easy."

Did he just threaten me?

Before I could find out, one of his goons pulled a gun and shot at Lyte, missing her by only inches and killing a bottle of vodka on the bar. I turned on him squeezing my trigger rapidly and hitting him twice in the chest. Calboy ran out from the other room he was in, using the cubby for a shield.

"What the fuck happen?" Calboy demanded to know, pushing the bloody man to the floor with the rest of them.

This wasn't the first time I had to kill somebody on a lick, but it was the first time I had to watch one die. Fuck it! It had to be done.

"Fuck this shit. Let's get outta here before them people

come. Ya know somebody heard all them shots," Lyte suggested as she grabbed the bag from the girl in the dress. "Get yo' ass on the floor now, bitch!" she ordered her with ice in her voice.

We backed our way out of the house.

As I made it to the exit, Papa stood up, poked his chest out, and then pointed his fingers at me as if he shot me with an invisible gun. I wish his bitch ass could see the smile on my face as I gave him a quick fuck you salute before I slammed the door behind me and ran to the getaway car sitting in the dark alley. Once I was in the backseat, Roc stomped on the gas and shot out of the alley. Lyte and I still ducked down in the seat until Roc got us far enough up Center Street and was sure we weren't being followed.

"We good. Y'all can get up!" Calboy informed us. "Now tell me what the fuck happened back there?"

I let Lyte do her thang and tell the story from her point of view, because I knew how bro could get when things didn't go as he planned them to. Yeah we were a team, but Calboy was our leader with no debate. I put my head back on the seat and focused on my breath to relax. I then closed my eyes, knowing this wasn't going to be the only conversation we'd have about the events that night.

TWO

KADEEM

"Good morning!" Mama Janet greeted as I walked through the daycare door to drop off my little ones.

Lovin' Care Child Care was on the corner of Congress and 37th. It belonged to Janet Wells, who was my late mother's best friend and my godmother.

Yeah, I lost my mom at a young age to the streets. She was shot and killed during a drive-by by a member of the Chicago gang known then as the B.O.S. (Brothas of Struggle) during their failed attempt to take control of Milwaukee's hoods. I was too young to remember the street war, but I know they lost, because it's now my stomping grounds.

"Good morning, ma."

I kissed her on the cheek.

"I might be late picking them up if them fools don't have Lady's car fixed."

"Okay! Since you think you might be late, just come by and pick them up at the house. I'm leaving early today anyways," she said as she walked over to the window. "Where's Ms. LaTrenda? Out in the car?"

I liked the way she asked questions that she'd then answer herself.

"Yeah! She on the phone with her daddy," I told her while watching her and my wifey exchange waves and air kisses. "I don't think Kie is feeling too good today. She's been crying on and off all night in her sleep. And Bull didn't eat this morning either. Lady checked their temp and all was good, so we don't know what's up."

"Boy, I got them. Go on and get outta here before that boy of yours comes back in here and sees you walking out the door. You know how he gets about you."

I did as I was told, knowing she was right about my son. I jogged back to my Tahoe, climbed inside and pulled off, and drove Lady to her job at the worst place in the city: The Milwaukee County Jail on 9th and State Streets. It was a straight shot south from the daycare.

"What's on your mind?" I asked, after noticing the frown on her face when she hung up with her dad.

"My daddy got robbed this morning, and my cousin Trey got shot up."

"Damn! That's fucked up! Is he okay? Do they know who did it?" I asked as we flowed down 12th Street.

"Daddy said he was shot three times in the chest, and they

6

still got Trey in surgery, so he don't know nothing yet." She wiped a tear from her cheek. "He don't know who robbed him either yet, but he ain't gonna stop looking until he finds the ones behind it. I don't know why he just won't let the police handle it. He's too old to be fucking around."

"Bae, ya know how he gets down. Yo daddy can't fuck with the police, but you're right that he is too old to be in the streets on this. Hey, and where's Chuck?" I asked, before I stopped at the red light on Highland Boulevard.

"He got pistol-whooped, but daddy says he's okay. I heard him talking shit in the background about what happened, but I really couldn't make out what he was saying."

The light changed and we were moving again.

"Is there something I can do, ya think?" I asked, pulling to a stop in front of the jail.

"I don't know! You know how they are. Just let them be, and if ya hear something about the robbery, let daddy know. I don't want you getting involved in their bullshit," she answered before opening the door to get out.

I love when Lady gets all fired up over something, but not shit like this.

"Ya don't gotta worry, ma. I won't. I'm about to be a married man, and I don't got time for all that wild, wild shit."

"That's right!" she agreed and then rewarded me with a kiss.

"You just have a good day and don't let them in there, or what yo' dad told you, stress you out too much."

"That's easy to say, but I'll try. Bae, don't forget to check on my car. I love spending time with you, but I need my ride back."

She then got out and stood holding the door open.

"Did you tell ma about the kids not eating?"

"Yeah, yeah. She said she got it and we gotta pick them up from her house. Look! There goes yo' friend—what's her face—waiting for you over there," I informed her while pointing at another nurse standing by the entrance.

Lady waved at her and then kissed me again. This time it was more to show off than to reward me, but I'd take it. I watched her walk all the way into the building and through the second set of doors before I pulled away. I didn't understand why they didn't have a different entrance than everybody else. I knew niggas be getting in their feelings talking about beating up nurses and COs and shit like it was their fault they fool asses got knocked. If they got on this money like me, didn't none of that petty shit matter!

THREE

GP

Me, Calboy, Roc, and Lyte met up with two of Cal's girls, Apple and Wonda. Wonda was not only his bottom bitch, but also his children's mother. We laughed our asses off watching the hysterically funny comedian Kevin Hart's stand-up show on Calboy's big screen as we counted up our take from the lick we did this morning. To be real with you, I was just glad we weren't still talking about how it went wrong. I swear if bro said one more word about that shit, I was gonna punch him dead in his big-ass lips.

"Geez, I got seventeen here!" I announced, after going over my calculations for the second time just to be sure.

"I got like ten and some change," Lyte said before she quickly got up, rushed to the bathroom, and slammed the door behind her.

"What's wrong with her ass? Is she sick or something?" Roc asked, just before he lit up one of the blunts he rolled from the six pounds of kush we got at afterset.

"Cal, you ain't gonna keep stressing my bitch the fuck out like ya been doing and shit, are ya?"

"Stay in yo lane, nigga! You know Lyte is super-touched emotionally. If ya can't handle her, give her back."

Wonda then got up from her seat.

"Daddy, I'ma gonna go see about her," she told Calboy before heading off toward the bathroom.

"Yeah, yeah, ma," he responded before turning back to Roc. "Nigga! Yo' ass might be a daddy," he jokingly teased in between laughing at the comedian.

"Naw, homey! I don't think she can get pregnant, because I been pounding that pussy out and filling her up with this super sperm since I first met her."

I couldn't believe he said that.

"That's just like a nigga. How come it gotta be her? Why can't it be that your soldiers don't march right?"

I couldn't wait to hear this answer.

"I know because my shit's good. Remember that snow bunny I used to fuck with?"

Roc must have read my eyes because he went on without my answer.

"That bitch got pregnant and lost it acting a fool at 618 when she got jumped by one of them hoes."

"Rocky! That hoe was lying to you. She wasn't pregnant; and if she was, it could've been anybody's! That bitch didn't get jumped by no hoes at that club. Her ex-boyfriend caught up with her and beat that ass for putting him in jail and running off with his cash."

I didn't want to hurt him, but it was time he knew the truth about Bonnie.

"What? Why ya just now telling me this shit?"

Ha ha! I think this nigga's mad.

"Look! Don't get mad at me. I'm just letting ya know."

"Yeah, don't get mad at sis. Yo' fool ass should fuck with the social media like everybody else and ya would've knew all this shit a long time ago."

Calboy took up for me as he plucked the burning blunt out of Roc's fingers.

"Bro, let me hit that?"

"Nope, bitch! Get yo' own," Roc snapped at me sitting on the edge of his seat.

Ha ha ha! Yep, he mad.

"I wasn't asking you. And it's all good, nigga. But I hope ya like catching the bus to the hood."

"Come on now, GP! Ya know I was playin'! That's how ya gonna do me?"

"Look at how ya came at me for telling you the truth and shit."

"I'm just saying ya should've told a nigga this shit a long time ago. I was helping the bitch with her rent and all that."

Roc was still explaining himself when Wonda walked back into the room with a very nervous-looking Lyte trailing her. Cal asked them if they were having a baby or not. And from the big smile that spread across Wonda's lips, I knew the answer.

"Well, bro, I gotta take back what I said. Yo punk-ass soldiers do work. They're just slow as a bitch!"

Everybody laughed with me.

"How do you know for sure?" he asked with a nervous look.

"We knew you was going to want to know that, so we took two tests."

Wonda handed Roc the two test strips and the box.

He read them and then dropped his head down onto his arms and knees.

"Are you mad? I'm sorry!" Lyte spoke up while fighting back tears.

When Roc looked up again he had the proudest smile on his face. He jumped out of his seat and hugged her.

"Naw, ma. I'm happy. I'ma be a daddy! I'm gonna be yo' baby daddy!" he sang while slowly rocking her in his arms.

The scene looked like something right out of a love story on the Lifetime channel.

~ ~ ~

Let's get back to what we were doing before all that goodness. Me and Roc sold weed. We'd split the loud pack and leave a pound for Calboy and them to enjoy. As always, Wonda and the kids got the odd money after each lick, since her only job now was to hold down things and turn the jewelry we acquired on our missions—as Calboy sometimes like to call them—into cash. Wonda would take the stuff to pawn shops up in Madison or Fon du Lac to get them off safely for us. As for the twenty-seven bandz of cash, Calboy and Lyte got nine each, but she had to give bro two grand because she was paying for her freedom. In case you haven't picked up on it, Calboy is also a pimp in his spare time. Anyway, me and Roc got $4,500 each. There were also two guns that we added to the armory that bro had been building up for the last few months.

"Say, Roc, ya ready to go home? Because I gotta get ready for school later," I said while putting on my powder-blue, iced-out Pelle coat.

I then tossed my backpack over my shoulder to make sure

he knew I meant now.

"Calboy, can you give us a ride home? I don't think Lyte's ready to go yet?"

"Yeah, I got you, since them three are gonna be talking baby talk for the rest of the day," Calboy shouted back, without taking a break from the war game that he was playing on the X-Box 360.

"Well, that's that. I'll catch up with you fools later!" I yelled into the kitchen to let the girls know I was going and that I'd call them after class.

~ ~ ~

For the first time on my drive home this morning I noticed how warm it was outside for it being mid-November. The first thing I did when I got home was put the money, weed, and gun in my secret place, and then I fed my best friend, Smoke. He is my cat that followed me home the first month I moved in, and he has never left my side since. I named him Smoke because of his off-white fur, and he likes to be right up under me when I'm smoking a blunt.

After a quick shower, I dressed in light blue jeans and my blue-and-white Milwaukee Career College sweatshirt. I raked down my wrap so I wouldn't look like a chicken head at school. I gave myself a quick once over in the mirror, refilled Smoke's water dish, and turned on the TV to keep him company while I was gone. I then pressed the remote start on my used black Porsche Cayenne while I put on my blue Nike Air Max boots. I made sure to grab my school bag before going out the door.

Last year I decided to get my GED. After getting it in just four months, I felt I could do anything. One of my teachers talked me into staying and going for my dream. So now I'm at MCC studying to become a veterinary surgeon.

<u>FOUR</u>

KADEEM

▌▌Man, why do I gotta drive in this shit? I'm sure it was yo turn, bruh," Gully said as he changed lanes to avoid having an accident.

"Look at that fool in that green F-150 that just hit that 'Lac. I'd have to burn that punk for fuckin' my shit up. Straight up!"

"Bruh, quit ya bitchin'! It ain't gonna be no better when I'm driving back. I told yo' ass to take 294 in the first place; and let's not forget it was you who wasn't ready this morning," I reminded him.

After I dropped off Lady at work, I went right to pick him up. He was the one still laid up with one of his many boopers that we had to drop off at home before we hit the highway to handle this business.

"No! We took that way last time, and we never take the same way back-to-back. And if I did go the 294 way, I'd have to drive through the city longer, and I hate that even more than this!"

"But it's home sweet home."

"Like I said before, bruh, just because I was born in Chi-town don't mean I like this muthafuckin' city!"

"Yeah, yeah, nigga! Just wake me up when we get there."

I turned up the Jamie Foxx radio show and closed my eyes, leaving him to deal with the stalled bumper-to-bumper traffic on 194 south. I'm sure I fell asleep, because the next time I opened my eyes, we were just a few blocks from our destination.

~ ~ ~

"Gully, we still got some time to burn, so let's run over to get some Jerks. I need some of them good-ol' Jerk chicken wings," I said, after looking at the time on my cell phone.

I called the plug to let him know we were there.

J. Ross didn't answer until the second call.

"Cool! I'ma meet ya at the park in say twenty-five to thirty minutes? It's all the same, right, fam?"

"Fo' sho, unless you wanna give us an early b-day gift today?"

"Ya know what? I just may be able to do that. Hit you in a few."

~ ~ ~

I ended the call, and Gully found a place to park when he made it over onto 79th. The line to Jerk was almost out the door. I didn't mind the wait since we had to kill time anyway. I passed time by playing Angry Birds on my phone. Gully passed it in the ear of a Windy City beauty. That's him. Always in a pretty face. Who could blame him? Gully is young, ghetto rich, and had the kinda roughneck swag that most women in our world liked. He stood around six foot three and worked out daily, making his 235-pound frame something most women couldn't keep their hands off of.

I'm not too bad looking myself. Gully often dragged me to the gym with him, so I could say I owed my five foot eleven, 200-pound hard body to him. But I won't. We met back in the early '90s. Both of us had gotten into enough trouble to land us at St. Charles Group Home. It was there where he adopted the moniker of Gully because he didn't feel Gilbert was gangsta enough, and it was him who gave me the name Wood, which I only used on the streets.

We then became brothers one Friday when I was on my way home for my very first weekend pass. I'd earned it by taking part in the nightly support groups held in the center. It took me a few weeks because I didn't feel like people needed to know my family business. But after a few lonely weekends there and punk-ass twelve-hour passes, I opened up some and they gave me a weekend pass. But not knowing what to do made me miss the bus, and not wanting to be anywhere around the group home, I started walking until the next city bus came along. That's when I came upon four shaved-headed, silly white boys surrounding one of the fellas from the group home.

I had seen him at St. Chucks a few times here and there, but we never talked to each other. I was still pretty new there, so I didn't have many friends nor did I want any. I just wanted to do my time and get home. I made eye contact with Gully, and his stare told me he needed help. I was fearless at five foot seven and about 145 pounds. I snatched a four-foot-long two-by-two stick from a nearby stack of wood on somebody's yard and ran up to the fight. I slammed it as hard as I could across the back of the first Skinhead son of a bitch that got in my path. My unwelcome surprise as well as the scream from the punk I had just hit, made the others take their eyes off of Gully. He didn't have any time to think, so Gully just started throwing hard right and left haymakers, hitting whoever was in his way. The Skinheads took off running, not expecting for things to turn out the way they had. That's how I met my best friend and got the moniker of Wood.

~ ~ ~

"Bruh, bruh! Ya ready to make this move?" I inquired.

About twenty minutes had passed since I talked to J. Ross. Gully then reluctantly excused himself from the woman and joined me.

It took Gully about ten minutes to get us to the apartment on the west side, which gave us time to slam down some food. One thing I learned is that he couldn't tell time or just didn't respect it. The nigga was either early or late, but always right on time with the product, and its quality was the best we had this close to home, so we couldn't complain.

"Shorty at Jerks was right! I may swing back down these ways to fuck with her in a few days."

"You mean fuck on her in a few days. She was thick as hell with a nice ass to go with it."

"She had a pretty face too, bruh," he added as we both laughed.

"She was a little more than all that. The short time we chopped it up, I could tell that shorty got a head on her shoulders to go with that pretty face," Gully spoke up in between bites of chicken.

"Oh shit! Let me find out ya got gamed by one of these Chi-town whores. Nigga, I'ma have to take a few playa points from you if ya keep talking like that," I teased before I ate a spoonful of brown rice and chased it with a bite of the spicy chicken.

"Naw, I think I'ma have to check the handbook to see if a nigga that's damn near married can do that," he countered. "She might be worth the loss."

I talk my shit, but I knew my partner really wanted a life like I have at home with Lady and the kids. I'm happy for him if he's real about it.

"I bet ya don't even remember her name. Come on, be quick with it."

"Alima Abdullah."

Damn! He might be serious remembering both her first and last names and shit.

"Is she Muslim with a name like that?"

"Oh, so now ya excited!"

"I'm not excited. It's just that we was right across from a masjid, and she could be."

"Yeah, she is. I think that's why I'm going to come at her on some real-real. I need a godly woman in my life."

"And maybe you would start back trying to learn the prayers like we made a deal to do if I worked out with you, remember? Or did ya forget that?"

"I didn't forget shit. I just didn't want to play with it when I wasn't really ready. Come on, bruh! Ya know I know you about that, and I'm not gonna disrespect."

"I feel ya. Now I don't wanna hear no mo' crying about driving down here now that ya met a pretty face."

My phone rang. I stopped talking shit to Gully and answered, since I knew that it was the plug.

"Put down the chicken, fam, and come up the street to the park. Pull right in by my whip, park, and then come watch the game with me," J. Ross instructed.

I agreed, and he then ended the call.

"What! He want another fifteen minutes or some shit?" Gully asked while slowing the car just a bit.

"Naw, he wants us to come to the park up the street and park right next to his Range and get out."

"Man, this nigga's forever changing his mind and shit. I guess it's how a kingpin lasts in this town."

Gully pulled back into the busy traffic.

"And back to what you said. I'm still not gonna like this muthafucka. I'll uproot Ms. Thang to the Mil if she's worth it."

I can't believe this thug is really talking about a relationship. I gotta meet this girl and find out what she said to him.

Gully then turned into the park, and it wasn't hard to find J. Ross's truck.

FIVE

KADEEM

J. Ross had a reputation for being unnecessarily vicious and highly competitive. He grew up on the bloody and grimy streets of the south side of the Windy City, where he ran dope packs for the neighborhood gangsters. All the while, he had dreams of all of it one day being his, so he could have the respect and power that he craved. So when the Feds did their sweep in the early '90s, young J. Ross didn't waste any time stepping up to fill the open position at the top in his hood.

Unlike the ones before him, he immediately got a few police officers on his payroll. J. Ross knew that by having some guys from the inside in his pocket, he could always be informed of any bust that was going down. This info allowed him to move in and take over other neighborhoods. It also made his crew, known as Young Gangstas, a force to be respected.

"Is it all there? I'm only asking because I'm about to make a move soon and need to know if I gotta come outta my pocket with any change," he asked, after waving us over to where he sat watching a junior football game with a few of his loyal workers.

It was clear to us they were really by his side as security.

"Did ya really think ya had to ask that? You know we're always on point with ours," I replied as Gully tapped my thigh to draw my attention to the parking lot.

We watched as two youngstas in their football gear switched the luggage from my Tahoe with the ones from the Range Rover.

"Any of them boys out there playing on the field one of yours?" Gully inquired, trying to make small talk until the kingpin gave the okay to hit the road.

"Naw! Gee, I just sponsor the team in black and gray. The way them fools are out there playing right now makes a nigga want a refund."

We laughed with him not knowing if he was serious or not.

"What's good with you? How's that music life treating you?" he asked Gully.

"It's all good, homey. I have a promising female singer doing her thang right now, and I just dropped a hot mixtape. It's in the truck right now."

"Alright, I hear you. I wanna check that shit out."

Right then one of his men came up and whispered something to him that I couldn't catch.

"Hey, just got some more B.I. to handle. I did toss a few extras in there for ya. On the next trip, I'll match whatever ya get."

"Hell yeah, that'll work."

We gave J. Ross a dap before we headed back to my truck. Once inside, Gully pulled off, only to make a U-turn about three blocks away.

"What? Why you turning around?"

"I forgot to give him a copy of my mixtape. Hell, I need all the help I can get to make this shit happen."

"I feel you. Ross might know Kanye or R. Kelly, for all we know."

"That's all I'm sayin'. Big as that nigga is, he gotta be the key to something besides them thangs."

When we got close to the park's entrance, we spotted the Range Rover surrounded by squad cars. J. Ross and a few of his men were all on their knees on the lightly snow-covered sidewalk.

"What the fuck happened that fast?" I questioned, seeing that my bro was just as surprised as I was.

"It looks like they just got hit in a raid at that house over there."

He pointed to a modest-looking house not far from them

as he crept along with the rest of the slow-moving onlookers.

"Bruh, them look like Feds."

I watched them walk more people out from the spot.

"Fuck this shit! I'm going around these fools. We don't need to be nowhere around this here. Shit! We don't know if them assholes seen us talking to Ross in the park or not."

"Go, go! I got the other set of license plates in the back. Find the first place ya can so we can swap them out."

Gully made a few quick left and right turns before stopping so we could change the plates on my Tahoe. Shit! A nigga wished we could change the color on this bitch too.

~ ~ ~

J. Ross saw us as we rode by, and his first thought was that we had set him up. But he wasn't the hood boss he was known to be by being a dummy. Before he jumped the gun, he would get as much info as he could before he ordered our deaths. Ross examined the faces of the officers not wearing blue FBI jackets and wondered why they weren't pre-warned. That's when he remembered an old head saying to him, "You think you big shit now because these toy cops don't fool with you, but know them Feds don't play fair with street cops."

Now he knew the old man was right, because the Feds had him and his team handcuffed on the sidewalk on display for all to see.

J. Ross's eyes searched for any other signs that would show him who the scoundrel was behind the raid. But when he was done scanning the crowd, his mind quickly returned to my truck as we sped away.

SIX

GP

I skipped my last class so I could go home and get some sleep before I took my ass into work tonight. Yeah, I got a job. What did ya think? I work at Lean's Foods, which were Milwaukee's Black-owned grocery stores. I liked my job because it was not far from my house on 17th and Capital. So I never feared being late if I had to hit that good old snooze button on my clock just one more time.

As always, old Smoke greeted me at the door as soon as I walked in. No, I'm not an old cat lady. I'm young. I'm only twenty-four, but I do wonder how it feels to have someone to come home to. Yeah, some days Smoke rubbing his fluffy self between my legs just isn't enough. He's certainly not enough when I want to be touched just a little further up, if ya know what I mean. Relationships are hard for me since I have real trust issues. I have good reason for my mistrust. I know I shouldn't aim my hate at all men because of one scumbag muthafucka that couldn't take no for an answer back in high school.

It happened during the back-to-school dance. I was sixteen

years old. I was small breasted, and I was slim but not too skinny and had a nice butt. Back then my long hair, light brown eyes, and even caramel skin tone made many of the boys pay attention. A big, coffee-brown skinned boy named Mike had a serious crush on me. Just like my cat Smoke, he would wait for me outside before and after school. Mike even paid a guy to switch seats with him so he could sit next to me in math class, which I found out was his strong point and not so much mine.

Mike had asked me out too many times to remember, and I turned him down every time. So when I decided to give in and call him to take me to the dance, he was so excited. He did his best to make everything so right for me. He was respectful at the dance. When we danced, he didn't try to grind all up on me like the other guys were doing with their dates. But then, those girls were into a lot more than I was at the time. We had fun dancing and talking about our peers from the year before and the new kids that were trying too hard to fit in.

"Gale, dance with me. I know good old Mikey don't mind. Do you?"

Mane was one of the school bullies and star basketball players. He was only asking me to dance to try to intimidate

Mike.

"No, I'm good. I'm tired and don't yo' rude ass see me talking to him," I responded smartly, rolling my eyes to let him know I wasn't feeling him not one bit.

"Oh, so that's how ya talk to a nigga? Well, when you ready for a real nigga to tap that right, come find me."

He smirked and then stepped on Mike's all-white Air Force Ones before walking away.

"What the? Damn! That nigga fucked my shit up!" Mike said while trying to wipe the dark smudges off with his hand. "If I wasn't with you right now, I would've put my hands on that dude!"

I could see he was very upset.

"Mike, you should try some of that hand soap in the bathroom. It should take that off," I told him, not knowing anything else to say.

"Yeah, all right! But don't go fuckin' with that punk when I leave. He's just mad that I'm here with you, and you're not hanging all over him like those airhead hoes over there with him now."

I saw Mane looking our way, so I gave Mike a little kiss on the lips that instantly changed his mood about his shoes. Mane shook his head and frowned at me. When Mike went to the bathroom to try to clean his shoes, I decided to go to the bathroom as well. I thought it would be better for Mike not to be alone and possibly let Mane bait him into a fight or something. But unknown to me, Mane had followed me to the bathroom. When I came out, he was hiding in one of the empty classrooms that I had to pass on the way back to the dance.

"Bitch, if ya scream I'ma cut yo' head off!" he whispered as he pressed something hard and sharp into my neck.

"Please don't hurt me. I'm sorry for talking to you sideways earlier," I begged.

His response was to throw punches at my head. He then slammed me to the floor and ripped open my leggings and rammed in me hard and uncaringly. I never thought my first time having sex would be at the hands of a monster. It felt nothing like what my girlfriends had told me about or how it was described in a romance book. This hurt. It hurt so bad that I must have passed out, because when I opened my eyes, I was alone on the cold floor.

That's where Mike found me.

"Gale! Gale! Oh shit! What happened?"

He could see that I was crying and that my clothes were all ripped and bloody.

"Help! Go get help!" he ordered one of the girls walking

31

by in the hallway. "Who did this to you, Gale? Who?"

"No, no, no, no! Just get away from me! Leave me alone!"
I fought Mike as he tried to help console me.

"Was it Mane, GP? Just tell me! Was it him?" he pled with
a rage in his eyes that I'll never forget.

Me crying harder was all the answer he needed. Once the
school staff arrived, Mike raced from the room in search of
the monster known as Mane. I was then taken to the hospital.

In fact, I was still in the hospital when I found out that
Mike was in jail for breaking Mane's jaw and beating him
within inches of his life with a chair for what he did to me.
That was just about seven years ago. Now the once innocent
little girl killed and robbed muthafuckas like that punk robbed
me of my pureness. Mike was sent to prison for twelve years
for what he did to Mane. I still stay in touch with him. I write
and send him money to show him how grateful I am and that
his sacrifice was not forgotten.

It's crazy how he got all that time and Mane's bitch ass
only got twenty-six months for what he did to me. Our laws
ain't shit! How could anyone think that these outcomes were
right? I used to think it was only in Wisconsin, but over the
years of helping Mike with his appeal, I found out it was like
that everywhere.

~ ~ ~

The sound of the ringtone I set for Calboy woke me up thirty minutes earlier than I needed to be.

"Damn! What ya want, man?" I snapped.

"Bitch! Fuck yo' sleep! Get up and open the door."

Bro started ringing my doorbell before I could ask him how long it was gonna take him to get here.

"Awwww! Why you ringing my goddamn doorbell like you crazy, punk?" I asked as I opened the door.

"Bitch! You know ya love to see me," he said as he walked in. "Do you got to go to work today?"

"Every day except Friday and Sunday. Why?"

I started getting myself ready for work since bro had gotten me up.

"I may have something sweet up for us. I'ma try to have Candi set it up tonight."

"Who or what is it?"

I was now fully dressed in my work uniform and putting food and water out for Smoke.

"It's a nigga named B—B. Burns. Candi says he's holding. He got to be on something to be fucking with them Cherry Street mob niggas. All of them getting money."

"He CSM?"

"Yup, one of the top figures. My lil' bitch says she's been to the nigga's crib somewhere off Goodhope. She got the address for me. All I need is you."

"Bro, let's not set this shit up for tonight. Tell Candi I want to holla at her when I get off work at six o'clock."

"Sis, what ya got on yo' mind? Do you know this nigga or some shit?"

"No! I just don't trust that bitch Candi's word for nothing, Cal. You know how she is about you. She's a dumb bitch. That nigga's maybe just a worker, for all we know. I bet she told ya about him to save her an ass whooping, didn't she?"

"Damn, girl! Ya talking like I'ma gorilla pimp or some shit. My bitches love me. If I went orangutan on a hoe where they'd fear me, I'd be in the same boat as the nigga I took most of them from."

"But you didn't answer my question, Cal."

After explaining my feelings about Candi to him for the umpteenth time, I headed out to work.

In case you're wondering why Calboy wanted to go on another lick so soon, it was definitely not that he didn't have money. Bro was far from hurting. He was just trying to get cash up so he could give us all a break and take a family vacation down to Disneyland or somewhere like that. His kids had been begging him to go, and his girls had been good to him like he said at my house earlier.

I'm on register tonight at work, so let me go find a Red Bull and get to it.

SEVEN

KADEEM

Back safely in the Brew City, the rest of the day was back-to-back to work. We couldn't get the dope outta the pot fast enough for the waiting crowd of hustlers we had in the spot. Gully was hard at work doing his magic, whipping up crack and sometimes doubling up what he dropped in the Pyrex pot. During that time, me and two of our loyal goons were working on weighing, re-rocking, and packaging it all up. I mixed and stretched the four extra bricks that J. Ross had fronted us, and turned them into six-and-a-half kilos, which I had already pretty much sold for $29,000 apiece. Gully turned the eight bricks we paid for into $17,000 and some. I'm not sure because he had this thing he did for his guys and their competition that we also did business with. His prices bounced between 25 and 30. His sold three and a half for an even 100 bandz right quick and another three for 65.

After helping him and KC clear the crowd outta the spot, me and Junior hit the streets to work on all the people on our lines who we had on hold. I sent Junior to set up the trap houses we had around the city with enough work to last them.

So he went one way and I went another. In the midst of all my running around, I almost forgot to run up to Wisconsin Muffler to pay for the repairs done to Lady's car, and then I was late going to pick her up from work. I felt bad as I raced through the streets toward the one place where I certainly did not need to get caught speeding around. I knew she was tired from work and the lack of sleep the night before because of the baby.

It was almost 3:00 p.m. when I made it to her. Lady and her friend Mary must have been out front waiting for me, because as soon as I pulled up, they were walking toward the truck. Lady put a smile on her face even though I knew she was mad at me being over a half hour late.

"Hey, luv!" I greeted her once she opened the passenger door. "Sorry I'm late. I got backed up at work."

She always laughed when I called what I do work.

"It's okay, bae. We didn't get off that long ago. Amy called a meeting at the last minute to address all the he-said, she-said bullshit going on in there. Bae, I told Mary we would give her a ride home since they don't got my car fixed yet, or did ya forget to check with them?"

"No! Yo' car is fixed. I just didn't have time to drop it off to you. But I did make it up there to pay for it on my way down here. Luv, my day has been rush-rush, for real."

"Awww, poor baby!" she teased.

She then followed it up with a kiss before I pulled away from the county jail.

We rode in silence for a second before they then got to talking about some weak-ass dude trying to kill himself by jumping off the upper level of one of the cell blocks. I knew they would start yapping about something. That's why I never turned back on my stereo. The two of them talked about everything from clothes to men.

"Bae, Mary wants to meet Gilbert." Lady smiled.

"Well, you got his number. Call him. Why ya telling me. I ain't the nigga's pimp."

"You ass," she joked and then playfully hit me. "I want to see what you think first."

"Mary, when did you see him?" I asked her, knowing that Gully didn't like to be nowhere near the jail and Lady was trying to play matchmaker in her spare time.

"I haven't! LaTrenda just told me about him."

"In that case, I think my other guy, KC, would be a better fit for ya than Gully, since she wants to play matchmaker and shit."

I turned on Lisban Avenue.

"Why you say that?" Lady asked, turning to face me in her seat.

"Gully met someone he seems to really be feeling."

It was that and bro didn't do full-figured women. I would hurt Mary's feelings by telling her that. I prayed they didn't press this with him harder. I knew if I asked, Gully would take one for the team. But Mary was good people, and I wouldn't hear the last of it from neither end.

"Oh, how come I'm just now hearing about this?"

I shrugged my shoulders, not wanting to keep talking about it.

"I thought KC had a girlfriend that he lived with?"

"What? That nigga been stopped fucking with old girl. Remember, she was the one that tried to fight with his mother?" I reminded her. "He been solo ever since. Mary, I'll give him yo' number. He's a good dude. Ain't got no baby mamas or no shit like that ya gotta put up with. He lives with mom, but he got everything else, and he's not there because he needs to be. KC just don't believe in paying for a place he wouldn't use," I explained, trying to sell her on him.

"He sounds like a winner to me. They say if a man treats his mother right, he'll treat his lady the same," Mary told me with a big smile at the thought of meeting a good dude.

I then turned into Wisconsin Muffler's parking lot and stopped next to Lady's cream-and-gold Buick LaCrosse.

"See! There ya go! All washed and shiny. Just the way ya like it ready for you and yo' buddy to hop in."

"Boy, if I didn't know better I'd think ya just told me to get outta yo' truck?" Lady said while gathering up her things.

"I guess ya don't, because that's exactly what I'm saying! Get the fuck out!" I said jokingly.

Even though we all laughed about it, I still got beat up by my girl before she got out.

I followed her down the street until I got close to my next customer that I had waiting on me until I took care of home. Ya know, happy home is a happy life. That's some real shit. That's why I try to make it a point to keep my girl smiling.

EIGHT

KADEEM/DETECTIVES

Deep in the heart of Cook County Jail, the two gung-ho arresting detectives went to work on their prizes.

"I'm Detective Dickerson, and this is my partner Detective Rodgers. Now you gentlemen are facing some serious charges."

"Stop right there, Dick. You fucked up when you called us gentlemen. Why don't you start by being real with us and say what's really on yo' minds."

"And what's that, Mr. Brown?" Rodgers probed.

"Nope! I think I'll let yo' Dick answer that for you."

Big Ed laughed. He always got a real kick out of teasing the detectives.

"See, that's why you people end up rotting away in prison with a boyfriend or beating your peckers or his for the rest of your sorry-ass lives. I was about to offer you assholes a good deal to put a word in for you with my good buddy who is the DA handling your case. But fuck that and fuck you!" Dickerson snapped.

"Ed, I think you struck a nerve. Here comes the old good-cop, bad-cop act that I bet these two got down to a science," Ross added, joining in on Ed's fun.

"You two sorry sons of bitches need to be smart for once and help us help you, James Ross and Edward Brown. Yeah, we know who you are, or who you think you are. We've been watching you for some time now."

"Give us the name of your suppliers, and that deal my partner was talking about is back on the table," Rodgers cut in.

Neither Ross nor Ed said another word. They just sat there with a you-can't-touch-me look on their faces. The detectives continued to take turns badgering them. Still getting the silent treatment, J. Ross knew they didn't have anything on them, because they wouldn't be wasting all this time trying to make them tell on themselves. After over an hour of questioning, which was more like talking to the walls, the detectives left the room. Moments later, an officer came in and took J. Ross out of the room. It was another ten minutes before the detectives returned.

"Look, Mr. Brown. We got off kind of rocky before, so let's start over," Dickerson started off as he and his partner took seats in front of Big Ed.

"Is there anything I can get you? Soda, water, coffee,

food?" Rodgers asked.

"Ya know what, you're right. We did get off on the wrong foot. Now that I think of it, there is something y'all can do for me."

"Okay, shoot!" Dickerson encouraged him, leaning forward with his pen and pad ready to write.

"Let me call my lawyer, and get the fuck outta my fuckin' face!" Big Ed laughed until Dickerson jumped out of his seat and grabbed him by the back of the neck and slammed his head down onto the cold, hard table.

Blood rushed from his busted lips and nose.

"Laugh at that, punk!" the detective yelled at him, before being pulled from the room by Rodgers.

"What the fuck was that? We can't let these punks get to us like that. You're in enough mess as it is. You don't need whatever high-priced lawyer these two are going to get slapping a suit on us. Now, let's let this one calm down, and get a smoke before we go talk to the other one. On second thought, you go and I'll do it alone."

Rodgers walked away from Dickerson and went right into the other room to try his luck with Ross.

J. Ross gave him the same answer that Big Ed had given him and asked for his lawyer. When the detective walked out of the room, he called an officer to come escort the men to the holding cell with the others. He thought that might loosen them up a little. On the way to the bullpen, Ross overheard Detective Dickerson talking to someone and telling them that they were going to have to bring in their CI from out of state. This made the heartless kingpin's mind return to my truck speeding away before he was tossed into the paddy wagon.

NINE

GP

After work I sat down with bro, and Candi's punk ass. I just didn't trust the bitch. She had a sneaky face. But I listened to her as she explained the layout of B. Burns's apartment.

"What number is he staying in?"

"I don't know. I was trying to memorize the address and forgot about it."

I could slap the shit outta this bitch.

"How yo' dumb ass gonna know the address but not the fuckin' apartment."

I am past annoyed with Candi's good-for-nothing ass.

"Sis, chill! This ain't shit to fix. Come on, bitch! Take us to his crib so we can know exactly where we're going," Calboy ordered.

I sat back in the car and let the hard bass of old-school Too Short's hit song "In the Ghetto" massage my body as I smoked some of that good kush we got earlier. This weed was so good I might have to pay that old dude another visit just to ask him for his connect.

"It's right down this street. Make a right at the corner," Candi spoke up from her seat in the back of Calboy's black-on-black Ford Crown Victoria.

"Bitch, I hope you right. Having me drive all the way the fuck up here!" Bro warned her in a very threatening tone.

I sat up and surveyed the area. Ya know, planning to fail because shit happens when it wants to, not when you want it to. So it pays to know all the escape routes of whatever territory you're in.

"Daddy, I am. I wasn't fucked up when he brought me out here with him. I was on my shit just like you taught me."

She shook her head like a little girl and then returned to face the window. It only took another five minutes to find the apartment, and I believe the only reason we did that is because Candi looked up and caught sight of B. Burns walking into his building.

Calboy found an adequate place to park.

"Now we just gotta find out what number he in."

A light went on in the lower left apartment window.

"Look! That light just came on. I'm betting that's the spot we need to be in," I said while pointing it out to bro.

"Do that look about right to you?"

"Awwww, yeah, daddy. I think so, because we didn't walk

up no steps. But I'm not all that sure because we went in through the back last night."

"If he usually parks in the back, that means he's gonna be running in and out. All we gotta do is chill and wait," he said while lighting up my unfinished blunt from the ashtray.

"It's right, daddy. You acting like GP. She never wants to believe me and always gives me a hard time and shit."

"Bitch, that's because you's a liar, and I know yo' ass would try anything to take Wonda's place at bro's side. But, bitch, until ya learn yo' place and hoe up the way you were brung on board to do, or woman up and stop selling yo' ass for another muthafucka, then I might have some respect for you. So shut up talking to me unless it's about getting this money."

Candi sat there with her head down thinking for a minute.

I was thinking the bitch might try me, until she asked, "Let me help y'all on this lick?"

"Ha, bitch! You so crazy."

I handed the last of the blunt to her. Here! Hit this and get yo' mind right."

"I'm so serious right now. I can make it easier by unlocking the door or a window when he comes to pick me up. Just let me help."

"Hold up, GP! My bitch might be on to something. Think about it. We can't just go kicking in the door without a muthafucka seeing us. What can it hurt to let her step up on this one?" Calboy suggested while putting out the Black & Mild he had just finished.

B. Burns walked out of the building, and I noticed the light in the apartment window was not off.

"Okay, Cal. It's on you if this shit gets fucked up because of her," I agreed as Calboy pulled off after the BMW.

"I'ma follow him just to see how he move. Who knows? We might luck up and come up on one of his stash spots," he explained in his lazy tone that let me know he was feeling the weed we had been smoking.

"Sounds good to me. Candi, I'm telling you now. Don't take nothing I do personal when we come in that bitch. If I don't make it look real, he might put two and two together and kill yo' ass for setting him up."

The look on her face told me that she hadn't thought about that part of it.

"Aww, girl! Don't look like that. We won't let shit happen to you," I told her, and then faced the front so she couldn't see the smile on my face.

"I know. I'm good. I was just thinking."

She sat back and stared out the window.

Following B. Burns took us to South Lawn projects where he parked behind a Cadillac CTS-V. He then opened the trunk before he got out. He walked up and started talking to the two men standing next to his CTS.

"Bro, do you know any of them niggas?"

"Yeah, the tall one is Annasta. She got that paper too. I know she's CSM. I can't see the other cat's face," Calboy answered as we watched B. Burns shake hands with them.

"I think that other one was at the last move we made. I'll know the name if I heard it."

"Oh yeah. That's Papa Luv."

"Yeah, that's it!" I said after hearing Candi say his name.

"He's an old-school pimp that's always trying to get at me when he see me in the club getting yo' money, daddy."

"Hoe, you better stay the fuck away from him," Calboy warned her. "Look at that there. Them two cats on the porch over there, GP."

I saw the house he was talking about just as one of them jogged over and put a duffel bag into the trunk of the BMW. We then pulled off after seeing this.

TEN

KADEEM

We stayed out late with the fellas at one of Papa Luv's aftersets trying to win back some of the five bandz I lost at the craps table. I then had to allow Lady to cash in on a no-work-day "Love Coupon" I had given her as part of a gift package for her last birthday to get out of the hot seat. Lady made sure I was punished by making me go shopping with her and the kids.

As I drove us to the Ashley Furniture store in South Milwaukee, we grooved to old-school Jay-Z's "Hard Knock Life," followed by the even older D.O.C.'s "Make It Funky." My son liked the bass that pounded out of the six 12" Rockford Fosgate subwoofers. Watching my little man bob his head through the rear-view mirror always put a smile on my face.

"I see you had this day all planned out whether I messed up last night or not," I said to Lady, who was pre-shopping in the store catalog.

"I sure did. We gotta get our time in with you somehow. Bae, what do ya think about this set right here?" she asked, and then held up the page so I could see it.

"It's okay, but there's always stuff in the store that they don't put in the catalogs that you're going to like, so don't ask me about something you know ya ain't gonna get."

"You don't know me!" She smiled. "You don't know me like ya think you do."

The parking lot was pretty empty, so I got a nice spot right up front. We were met inside by an eager sales rep. Don't get me wrong! I don't mind furniture shopping. The stuff at the house was long overdue to be replaced, in my book. The kids had done everything from throw up on it to try to kill it by stabbing it with a fork or two. We also had it for over a year now, which was a record for Lady. She usually only kept a living room set for six months and then sold it to a friend or family member. But I guess she changed her spending habits some with our growing family.

After being in the store about twenty minutes, give or take, I found a black, iron-and-gray marble three-piece table set that I liked.

"Bae, if you like that, we can get it. But I didn't see nothing in the catalog that looked good to me that matched it, so now I gotta look for something."

"You were going to do that anyway if I picked this out or

not, so don't try to make it seem like it's on me that ya can't make up yo' mind," I told her as I followed her with my son sitting on my shoulders.

"It was a nice try, wasn't it?" She laughed and wandered off to look at the children's bedroom sets that we didn't need.

"I'm not paying for that. We don't need it, so don't ask."

"I didn't ask you to, ya meany! I was just looking."

Another thirty minutes passed before Lady settled on a five-piece living room set with ash-gray upholstery. I got the salesman to throw in free stain guard for life, and we had a deal. My work phone started ringing.

"Uh oh! Daddy's gotta go to work, mama!" my son informed Lady at the sound of Yo Gotti's song "Touch Down," which I used as a ringtone for my text messages.

I looked at the screen and saw the text was from Annasta—*I need to see you ten times ASAP. Bread on the table.*

Without a second thought, I hit her back telling her I was on my way. I didn't notice Lady standing over my shoulder.

"Now why did you just lie to them?"

"What you mean?"

"You know what, nigga? Don't play dumb."

"Lady, this is twenty-two racks ya asking me to pass up,

after you just spent over eight up in here. Bae, we need that!" I pleaded.

"I know! I know. And I ain't never going to make you pass that up, but you promised me, so after you handle that, no more working. This is our day."

I agreed with her, paid for the new furniture, and then drove her and the kids home where Lady loaded them right into her car.

"I'm going to Walmart. Be here when I get back, or else," she threatened.

I called ahead so I wouldn't have to get out of my truck.

"Put ten whole ones together for me, bro-bro. I'ma be there in five," I told KC, referring to the weed order I had online for Annasta.

I pulled up out back of the safe house and hit my horn two quick times. KC came right out carrying a duffle bag.

"I need ya to drop off two to my OG for me at Mom's crib," he said as he climbed into the truck.

"I got you. Do I gotta grab that cash from him or you gonna get it later?"

"I got it already. He's just waiting on us."

"Alright, how things going around here?"

"Shit's busy as hell on all sides. Just the way ya like it.

This is why I couldn't get to my pops right away."

"Well, have fun. It's all you. Lady still got me on lockdown with her and the kids for the day. She only let me out now because I told her how much bread was on the line."

"Hey, y'all should come out with me and her buddy tonight. She wants go to open mic night at Brooklyn's."

"Only if ya gonna get up there and show off yo' skills for us."

"I might, I don't know yet. Ya just gotta come to find out."

"I'ma see if Lady wants to go, and then I'll hit ya with a text."

We dapped up, and then he got out and ran back into the house.

~ ~ ~

Ten minutes later I was pulling up to Annasta's spot. Now here was the thing about Annasta: she was a lesbian and looked like a man from the low-brush cut waves in her hair down to her stocky build. The only thing that gave her away was her voice. I met her through Lady's dad awhile back when she lost her weed connect, and we'd been jammin' ever since. It was her girlfriend that she bought the weed for.

Annasta moved more bricks than me and Gully ever did.

We never shopped with her or any other member of the Cherry Street Mob, but I was really considering it now that J. Ross got knocked. Before I went her route and paid her high-ass numbers, I'd see what my down south connect was talking like. In the past, their drug prices were always worth the trip. The only reason we slowed up on them was because J. Ross's prices weren't that much higher and the dope was just as good, and only a little over an hour away instead of fifteen.

After leaving Annasta, I called Lady to find out where she and my babies were. To my surprise, she was home asking me if I felt like going out with Mary and KC.

"He just asked me that when I seen him, so if ya wanna go it's all good with me."

"Okay, bae. I still got Mary on the other line, so I'll talk to you when you get here."

"Hey, pick me out something to wear."

She told me she was already working on that, and ended the call. I put my cell on the car charger and then let Miltown's Baby Drew pound hard as I rapped along to his gangster lyrics.

ELEVEN

KADEEM/GULLY

Once the day had slowed down for Gully, he made his way home to his Highland Park apartment. He didn't believe in moving out of the hood. Gully had to be close to the action at all times. I also lived on Highland Boulevard, but just not down in the hood. I was in the high numbers mostly surrounded by homeowners like myself.

Gully was met at the door by his red-nosed pit bull, Killa.

"Did you miss me? Yeah, you did, and I bet ya ready to go outside?"

At the mention of the outdoors, Killa ran and got his leash and dropped it at Gully's feet. Gully picked it up and then tossed the backpack he was carrying onto a dining room chair. He then grabbed a beer from the fridge and took his dog out for a walk. Gully enjoyed the walks as much as his dog did, because they allowed him to flirt with a few of the girls in the hood and make sure our runners and watchers were on point with their jobs.

After spending about an hour outside, they made their way back into the apartment. While Killa busied himself with his chew toy, Gully dumped the backpack onto the table and sat down with a fresh beer to sort and count the money he picked up on his rounds. Five minutes into his count, Alima popped into his mind, so he decided to call her.

"Hello, sweetie. How ya doing?" she answered cheerfully.

"I'm good. Did I catch you at a bad time. Ya sound busy," he said, hearing the sound of pots and pans banging around in the background.

"No, not really. I'm just helping my granny with dinner, but I can still talk now. Now, mister, what happened to you? I've been waiting to talk to you ever since you said you were going to call me back yesterday," Alima inquired as she chopped vegetables for the salad that she was preparing.

"My bad, love. My bro's wifey put him on punishment for hanging out late with the fellas, so I got real busy. By the time things slowed down for me, it was late and I couldn't remember what time ya said you went to work," he answered while banding out $5,000 all in $10 bills.

"I'm a grown-ass woman, Gully! I can talk late on the phone if I want. I pay this bill." She let out a little laugh. "I'm at work right now. I take care of my grandparents. Something you would know had you asked."

"I would've got around to it sooner or later, but I be so

high I'm surprised I remembered talking to you at all."

"I'm not sure how to accept that," she joked back as she put ground turkey into a pot on the stove.

There was a moment of silence that made her think the call was disconnected.

"Hello?"

"I'm here. I just lost my count. I heard ya though. You shouldn't take nothing I say in a bad way. So tell me, when can I see you again?"

"Ya can see me right now. I'm gonna send you a picture."

"That's not what I'm talking about. I'm saying person-to-person contact."

He finished banding another five G's.

"Oh, well, you're the busy one. When can you come down here? I can take off whenever I want. These two are always happy to get rid of me around here."

"I can be there tomorrow night if ya want me. I mean, want to see me."

"I don't know. I think you meant it just how ya said it the first time."

"Would I be wrong?"

"Come on down, and we can address right and wrong just as ya say, person to person."

Gully could hear the smile in her voice. He found her calming and easy to talk to. He set the date for the next night.

"Now, don't forget to send that hot shot," he reminded her before ending the call.

I guess I'ma have to miss him for a day or two. But I'm happy for him. It's about damn time he found someone to be real about.

TWELVE

GP

We followed the BMW from Goldstar Gentlemen's club. It's the strip club Candi liked to work in when she didn't have any out-of-town bookings. Right now she was in the car with B. Burns. We watched them pull in and park behind the apartment just the way she said he did. We could see them clearly from where we had parked in front so we wouldn't spook him.

"Let's wait until they get inside before we make our move. There are a few lights on in the building next door that concern me," I said as I pointed them out to Calboy and Wonda.

"I thought that was the plan in the first place?" Wonda asked.

"It is."

I fished me a pair of black latex gloves outta the box that we brought from the house.

"So, what made you say that just now? You think I forgot how this shit works or something?"

"No, I just know how bro thinks."

"I was sho' on some *walk the nigga in the house* shit until

I seen that," Calboy confirmed as B. Burns walked his sucka ass round to open the door for Candi to get out of the car.

The short, short skirt showed off her long legs and maybe even gave him a sneak peek at what was to come.

"Cal, how come you don't open the door for me like that?"

"Wonda, don't disrespect my thuggery by asking me no shit like that. We been fucking with each other way too long for ya to get on that bullshit. Ya know it's true thug pimpin' with me all the time and all the way," he reminded her as he pulled on a pair of gloves as well.

"I know, but a bitch can always dream, can't she?" she said while climbing into the front seat behind the wheel and getting ready to make a quick getaway once we came out of the building.

B. Burns stood about six-foot tall, with a potbelly, and a nasty-looking scar running along the right side of his face. It was given to him by his baby mama after she caught him getting sucked off by her dope-head mother. But even without the scar, it would be hard for him to get with a female as good looking as Candi.

The lights soon went out in the apartment, which was our cue to move.

Calboy, Roc, and I got out of the minivan, crossed the

street, and walked in the shadows until we were around the back of the building. Calboy checked the kitchen window and found it unlocked. I was shocked that Candi was actually doing her job. Since I was the smallest, I climbed through the window and opened the door for them. We took out our guns and pulled down our masks before moving farther into the dark of the apartment. All we had to do was follow the moaning and grunting to find the bedroom on the left of the bathroom. I slowly pushed open the door and saw Candi on top.

"That's it, that's it! Oooh shit! That's it, baby! That's how daddy likes it!" B. Burns told her, slapping her hard on her ass a few times.

I swiftly walked over to the bed and broke his nose with my gun. He screamed.

"Shut the fuck up!" I snapped, hitting him again and kicking Candi to the floor to make it look good for her.

"All we want is the money and the work, and nobody's gotta die in this bitch!" Calboy told him while rummaging through the bedroom.

"I ain't got shit here!" B. Burns lied.

"Wrong answer, bitch!" Calboy punched him twice in the face. "Now where the hell is the shit at?"

"Okay, okay! It's in the front closet on the floor. The code is 10-40. Please don't hit me again?"

Roc walked into the closet to find the safe. Bro didn't find much in the room but a few iced out rose-gold pieces that Wonda would love to get her hands on. I went to look elsewhere. Calboy found a .357 Mag on the nightstand. After Roc cleared out the money from the safe, he walked back into the room.

"Where's the work at?" he demanded.

"That's all I got; I swear to God. On my life, that's all I got in here."

His words made Calboy think back to the first day we followed him.

"G, get the nigga's car keys and go look in the trunk," he told me.

I did as I was told; but as soon as I got the bag outta the trunk and ran it to the van with Wonda, I heard gunfire. I rushed back to the apartment. But by the time I was halfway there, Roc and Calboy were running toward me. They were being chased by another man shooting wildly at them.

I made it back to the van and jumped in the back. I returned fire at the man, who ducked off behind a parked car. Calboy made it into the van, but Roc got shot. I heard him scream out in pain. Wonda pulled the van over to where he fell in the street. I took her gun and kept the gunman pinned down while bro jumped out and pulled Roc into the van.

"Is it bad? Is he alive?" both me and Wonda asked as she stormed down the street.

"He's knocked out, but he's still breathing. Turn on the light so I can see where he's hit at!" Calboy ordered her.

I climbed over to help him. Roc was shot twice, from what I could see—once in the leg and again in his lower back.

"We gotta get him to the hospital right away," I told Wonda, taking off my black tee and tying it around the wound in his leg.

"We can't go straight to the hospital, because they're gonna know we had something to do with that shootout over there."

"What y'all want me to do then?" Wonda asked, still racing toward the hospital.

"Slow down! Slow down!" I yelled at her.

"Take us on 49th and Locus and let us out. Sis, we gonna get out and bust a few times in the air around there so she can run him to St. Joes."

"Okay."

I collected the bags and got ready to move as soon as

Wonda got us where bro told her to take us to.

"Let us out here. As soon as you hear us shooting, drive around to the emergency room and get him help. Tell them he was shot as he was getting into the van or some shit."

Me and Calboy got out and ran down the blocks toward Center Street, shooting into the air. Then he stole a car and drove us to his house. We parked the car on the next block and then whipped it down while making sure not to leave prints. We then made it into the house to wait for Wonda's call.

"Fuck Gale! I fuckin' forgot my cell in the van. I hope Wonda thinks to call you."

"She's pretty shaken up, so if you don't answer when she calls, ya know she's gonna call me. Now what happened in there? Where did dude come from?" I asked, sitting down on a dining room chair at the table.

"I guess he was in the other bedroom across from us. All I know is that I turned in time to see him trying to creep up on us. I yelled for him to drop his gun, but the fool shot instead. So me and Roc shot our way to the front door with the nigga on our ass."

"Ya see, that's what I was talking about. How did that bitch not know there was another muthafucka in that bitch? I started to go into that room before I went to check the car, but didn't because of how long we been in there already."

I put my head down in my hands as I explained. Bro walked up behind me and handed me a beer.

"It's not yo' fault, GP. I ain't no fool. That bitch knew there was somebody else in there and just didn't tell us because she was scared or some shit. I'ma beat the shit outta her when her punk ass gets here."

"Calvin, do ya got something to smoke? I need to calm my nerves."

I took a swallow of the cold beer.

"Shit! I better call Lyte and tell her what happened, so she can go to the hospital with them."

I picked up my cell phone off the table.

"Yeah, ya know she's worried because we ain't called her yet. I don't want her ass going through there looking for us," he said, tossing a box of blunts onto the table along with a nice-size baggie of weed. "I hope that nigga makes it."

In the middle of placing the call to Lyte, I got an incoming call from an unknown number. I usually don't answer numbers that are blocked or don't look right to me, but I had to because it could be Wonda.

"Who is this?" I demanded when answering the call.

"This is Wonda, GP. Is Calvin with you? He's not

answering the phone."

"Yeah, he's right here. He forgot his phone in the van. How's Roc doing?"

"Is that Wonda?" Calboy asked.

I nodded my head yes.

"I ain't heard nothing yet. I'm in the family room waiting," she explained.

I could hear the worry and stress in her voice.

"Hold on! Lyte's trying to call me back." She agreed, and then I switched over. "Hello?"

"What's wrong, GP? You called and hung up on me."

"I didn't hang up. Wonda called. But Lyte, Roc just got admitted at the ER at St. Joe's."

"What happened? Is he okay?"

"I don't know. We ain't heard nothing yet. Wonda is there with him now."

"Stop talking to me like I'm a kid. What happened?"

"I can't say exactly, but he was caught up in the crossfire of a shootout. That's all I can say on this phone. Ya need to get up there with Wonda just in case they need some info on him that she don't know. My bro will be there in a few hours, okay?"

"Alright, alright. Tell her I'm on my way."

Lyte hung up to get dressed and rush to the hospital. I then switched back to my other line.

"Wonda?"

"I'm still here."

"Lyte's on her way there. Here you go, bro."

I passed him the phone and took the blunt out of his fingers.

I needed something to do, so I reloaded the guns. When I was done with that, I took a look in the duffel bag that I took from the BMW. It was mostly cash, but also had some dope in the mix. I'd never sold cocaine before, but I knew enough about it from being around Roc and Calboy. There looked to be around three keys in the bag.

Calboy looked over at me as I set the dope out on the table.

"How much is there?" he asked excitedly.

"Just this. The rest is money."

I picked up the rubber-banded stacks of cash for him to see.

"What are y'all talking about?" Wonda asked him.

"I was talking to GP about what was in the bag. My bad! I'm listening to you."

"I don't think ya can call my cell in here, so just text me and I'll call you back from this phone."

"Alright! I'll have sis text you when we on our way up there. Call us back as soon as you hear something from the doctors."

They said their goodbyes and ended the call. Then he sat down to help me kill time counting the take from the robbery.

~ ~ ~

When Lyte pulled up outside of the emergency room entrance, she could see the waiting area was crowded as always. Paramedics were bringing gurneys inside left and right while doctors and nurses ran from room to room. Lyte found a nurse to show her to the family waiting room. As they walked down the halls, Lyte heard her name being called.

"Have you heard anything yet?" she asked Wonda with a quick hug.

"No, nothing yet."

"Where is he? Do you know what room he's in?"

"Yeah, he's down here."

Wonda escorted her to the room, where the two of them looked through the window at several medical personnel working hard to save Roc's life.

"Excuse me? You two can't be here. You're going to have to go back to the waiting room until someone comes for you," a tired-looking nurse said before she closed the room curtains on them.

Wonda and Lyte returned to the waiting area after getting a cup of coffee. They spent the next hour without another word being told to them about his condition. Wonda told her about the shooting and why the rest of us weren't at the hospital. But she knew the game and understood the reason.

Lyte put her head down and said a quick prayer for the father of her unborn child. Wonda closed her eyes and also prayed for her friend. Another hour passed before a doctor came in and told them that they could go and see Roc. When they walked into the recovery room, he was still asleep from the meds. Wonda texted me and told me that he was okay. I replied and let them know that we'd be there shortly.

THIRTEEN

ANNASTA

▲▲Sis, Marcus got shot. I'm on my way to the hospital with him now," B. Burns explained to Annasta as he watched his eighteen-year-old son being strapped to the gurney.

"What happened? Who shot him?"

"Somebody ran up in my apartment. I can't really explain right now."

"Sir, you have to get off the phone and put on your seatbelt or get out so we can go," the paramedic told B. Burns as he took a look at B. Burns's facial wounds.

"There's a girl here named Candi. When you get here, she can tell you what went down. I gotta get off the phone. Come over here with her so you can keep these police in their place in my shit. I'ma call you as soon as I can."

One of the other paramedics, that was finished with Marcus, then checked to make sure B. Burns was locked in the wall seat before they pulled away.

"We're all set back here. Let's roll!" the paramedic called out to the driver.

~ ~ ~

Annasta started getting dressed.

"Baby, what you doing? Where you going?" Marci asked while awakening from her lover's movements in the bed.

"Marcus got shot. B's on his way to the hospital with him now. I got to go to his place with the police so I can keep them in check. Lord knows what he got stashed in that bitch."

"Baby, yo' hands are shaking. You should let me drive you," she offered, already getting dressed.

"Alright. Hurry the fuck up!" Annasta told her, picking up her gun and pressing the remote start on her keys.

Once she heard the loud pipes of her Lincoln Navigator roar to life, she grabbed her clothes on the way to the bathroom.

"After dressing, Marci pulled the truck out so they could pull right off when Annasta came out.

~ ~ ~

When the ambulance drove away, Candi walked back into the apartment. She was looking around for her cell phone, when she remembered that B. Burns had made her leave it in the car. She went back outside and walked over to the BMW with its trunk still open from the robbery. When she closed it and found the keys still in it, she also noticed two police detectives walking her way, so she quickly pressed the unlock button on the remote, opened the door, and got her bag out of the backseat. She then made sure to arm the car alarm, which locked all the doors.

"Miss, miss! Is this your car?" one of the detectives asked, already knowing the answer.

"No, it's my boyfriend's. Why?"

She noticed that they had split up to approach her from both sides. Candi slowly backed away from them.

"We were told that the owner may have something to do with the shooting that took place here. Is that true?"

They cut her off midway to the door of the apartment.

"He didn't have nothing to do with it. His son was the one shot. If y'all wanna talk to him, they're on their way to the hospital."

She tried to walk away, but the detective closest to her grabbed her by the arm.

"Hold up. We're not through with you just yet."

"I'm not going nowhere, but it's cold out here," Candi said, hugging herself from the morning chill.

The cunning detectives used the cold as an opportunity to get inside the apartment and snoop around.

"Let's step inside and finish this," Detective Webb suggested.

Candi didn't see a way around letting them inside. She knew she really didn't have a say so about what they could and couldn't do once they were inside, because it wasn't her place. She thought of going back to sit in the car, but they noticed that she had left the patio door open and they were already walking her back in that direction.

"How long will this take, because I really need to get to the hospital with them?" she lied, having no intention to go to the hospital.

She was really only going to hook up with her pimp and make sure he was okay.

I met up with them as soon as they walked through the doors. Marci and I came in through the front door moments before.

"What's going on here?" I asked the first detective that stepped into the kitchen.

"That's what we're here to find out. Let's start with you telling us who you are," Webb said.

"This is my brother's place. He called me to come lock up the place. So if you don't have a warrant."

"No, we don't have a warrant. We were just stepping in

74

out of the cold with your brother's girlfriend here. But from the looks of this place, we don't need one."

"Why is that?" Marci asked.

"It looks to be part of the crime scene," the second officer said, stepping from behind Candi. "Now, ladies, please have a seat and let's see some IDs."

They did as the detectives had asked.

After answering all of their questions, I had no choice but to allow the CSI team to come in and take photos, and to collect shell casings and slugs from the walls where the gunfight had occurred.

"Look at what we found here," Detective Benson said when one of the men found half a pound of weed and a large amount of cash in my nephew's room.

"I don't know shit about that. But let me call my lawyer to handle all this shit from here on out."

I knew how careless my brother was. B didn't play by the rules of the game, such as Rule #3: Never have shit where you lay your head.

Once the detectives and their team finished up and cleared out of the apartment with a strong promise to return, I had a talk with Ms. Candi. I needed to know what really went on. The bitch seemed very nervous. I could tell she was lying to the cops about being in the bathroom hiding when the shooting started.

"As soon as we got into the house, we went straight to bed. Maybe thirty minutes or so later, someone busted into the bedroom and kicked me to the floor. Then they kept hitting B in the face."

"Did you see any of their faces?" I asked, standing over her as she recapped the events of the robbery.

"No! They had on masks, and I don't know how many there were because there was someone in here," Candi answered, referring to the living room where we were now.

"What else happened?" Marci questioned suspiciously, standing across from me.

"Like I said, they kept hitting him until he told them where the stuff was. The next thing I know, what's his name popped outta that room yelling for the niggas to drop their guns. But the one I couldn't see in here shot at him and missed. Then the two of them ran out the door, and he chased them outside. B grabbed a gun and followed them. All I heard next was a bunch of shooting and a car smashing off. I stayed in the room on the floor until I heard B call to me and tell me to call 9-1-1 and tell them his son got shot."

"So ya didn't see shit that can help me find out who this

was?" I asked her, showing the frustration in my voice.

"Nope! They all had on masks, and after seeing the way they beat up on B, I just kept my head down like they told me to," Candi explained before she lit the cigarette she had been holding in her fingers.

I could see the smoke settling her after she took her second pull.

Marci's mind had been racing ever since she laid eyes on Candi.

"Bae, can I talk to you in the kitchen right quick?"

"What up?" I asked when we were away from Candi.

"I know that bitch from when I worked that club in Iowa."

"So!"

"She fucked with this pimp nigga Calboy that's known for doing shit like this. I bet she set B up."

"Let's go ask her and find out."

I walked back into the living room where Candi was still sitting and smoking her cigarette. I hoped B wasn't trying to wife this bitch, because he was gonna be mad at me.

"I hope they alright. He said he was gonna call when they got to the hospital," Candi lied while putting out her smoke.

"He might have gotten held up by them nosey-ass police. They said that they was going to talk with him. Don't get surprised if he gets locked the fuck up for that shit they found in here!" I told her.

"Say, don't ya know a nigga named Calboy?" Marci asked her.

At the sound of the name, Candi's facial expression changed.

"I—I used to talk to someone they call that, but I don't no mo'," she answered thinking quickly. "Why you ask?"

I pull my gun and pointed it in her face.

"Bitch! You set my brother up and got my nephew shot, didn't you?" I demanded.

"What! No, no! I—I don't know nothing about this. I swear to God, I don't know!"

"She's lying, bae. I can see it in her face."

"Fuck you, bitch! Ya don't know me to be saying shit about me!" Candi snapped back at Marci.

I instantly punched her in the mouth and busted her lip. "Ya lying-ass bitch! Where that hoe-ass nigga live at? Tell me where he live and I won't kill yo' fool ass up in here!"

"I don't know what!"

I cut her lie off with my hard fist. She fell back on the leather sofa and tried to cover her face as we rained down enraged blows on her head and wherever else they landed.

"Okay, okay! Please stop! I'll tell you!" Candi cried over and over, trying to make us stop hitting her.

After giving her a well-whopped ass, she told me just what I wanted to know, but she still denied having anything to do with the setup. I got on the phone and called my young shooters.

"Get shit together. We got shit to go handle."

"Is it like that like that, or just some foot-to-ass shit?"

"No! This here is real. I'll be there in a few," I told them before ending the call.

Whether this bitch was lying or not, somebody was gonna feel my pain.

FOURTEEN

GP

At 7:48 a.m., a cab pulled up to Calboy's house on 48th and Wright Street. A woman got out and hurried to the door and then rang the bell.

"GP, get the door. That should be Candi," Calboy called out from the bathroom.

"Alright."

I got up from the table where I was busy dividing the money, when a funny feeling came over me. I grabbed my gun and walked over to the door, just as the doorbell rang again.

"Who is it?" I questioned before I looked out the peephole.

"Apple."

I opened the door and let her in.

"What's up, girl!" I said as we hugged.

"I thought you wasn't coming back 'til tomorrow some time?"

"I was, but I busted a move on a lame-ass nigga for a few racks, and a bitch had to get on the first thing smoking outta there. Shit was slow up there anyway." She took her coat off at the same time and then stared at the money and drugs on the dining room table. "I see I ain't the only one that's been busting moves around this bitch." Apple then turned to me. "Where is everybody? GP, is that blood on you?"

I had been so worried about Roc that I didn't think to change out of my bloody clothes.

"Bitch, what you doing back right now?" Calboy barked at her when he walked back into the room dressed in fresh clothes.

"Daddy, don't be like that. I hit this nigga for ten G's and had to get the fuck outta there fast. I thought ya sent me out to get money, not play games," she explained, pulling the money out of her handbag while smiling as she handed it to him.

"That's my bitch!"

He hugged her and then kissed her on the forehead.

"Shit must've been slow, or do ya got another booking somewhere else set up?"

"Both! I had Creamy book me where she's at. I texted all this to you. You didn't get it?"

"I forgot my phone in the van with Wonda, but it's all good, ma. Don't trip."

"Now, what happen here? Why do GP got blood on her?"

"Shit! This lick we went on went bad, and Roc got shot."

"Oh my God! Is he okay? Where's Wonda?" Apple

interrupted him fearing the worst.

"We don't know yet. Wonda had to rush him to the hospital. As soon as I get changed, we going up there, so ya right on time. I need to borrow something to put on," I told her.

"Ya didn't have to ask me to do that. Ya know what's mine is yours. Go right ahead. I got jeans and sweats in my carry-on."

Apple handed me the key to the lock on her bag.

"Cal, can I go to the hospital with y'all?"

"As a matter of fact, I need ya to go up there with GP 'cause I gotta wait here for Candi. I ain't heard from her yet, and I've been texting her from GP's phone."

"Okay. What that hoe do?"

"She helped us on the lick. I don't know if she got shot in the midst of things or what."

Bro's face showed his concern as he explained.

"What? You let her dumb ass go on a lick with y'all?" Apple asked in shock, because everybody knew how scary Candi could be.

"She put the shit together. She got to fuckin' with that ugly-ass nigga B. Burns and put us on him," I explained to her as I grabbed a T-shirt and blue jeans from her bag before heading into the bathroom to get cleaned up and changed.

After seeing myself in the mirror, I decided to take a quick shower. I stripped out of the bloody clothes and stepped under the hot water. As soon as I did, the feeling I had earlier returned, but I just blew it off as nervousness.

A few moments later, I heard the doorbell followed by gunshots. I fell out of the shower, got up, and ran out into the front room naked. There, I came face-to-face with two dread-headed goons standing over Calboy's body in the doorway. I saw a gun on the table and ran for it. They shot at me and then turned to run back out the door, but not before I shot one of them in the back as I unloaded the clip in their direction. I slipped and fell hard on the floor, just as a storm of bullets ripped through the wall and big front windows.

I covered my head and stayed on the cold floor until I heard a car speed off. When I looked up toward the door, I was met by bro's lifeless eyes. He was on top of Apple, who I thought was also dead until I heard crying and moaning in pain. I made my way over to them.

"You okay? Apple, where are you hit?" I asked her while rolling Calboy off of her.

"God no! GP, is he dead? Tell me he's not dead," she cried, sitting up and leaning back against the door frame.

The tears running down my face said it all as I shook my head yes.

"Help me pull him in so we can close the door."

Apple just sat there hugging herself crying.

"Apple! Get the fuck up and help me with him. We gotta get you to a hospital, and we got to get everything outta this house before the police get here."

"Okay, okay, okay! I'm good."

She then helped me pull him inside and shut the door.

I took her into the bathroom, but not before I grabbed another gun from the table. She had a deep cut on her forearm that needed stitches, but she wasn't shot. I wrapped it with my old shirt, and then we went through the house collecting guns, cash, and drugs and putting it in the trunk of my car after I got dressed.

I then made a call to 9-1-1, even though we could already hear the police coming.

I left the gun that I shot the dread-head with on the floor for when the police asked what had happened. Apple was so shaken up that I had to make sure she only told them what happened, and none of what we told her about the robbery we did earlier.

The house was soon filled with police.

"Excuse me, ma'am. I know it's hard, but I need you to tell us what happened here. I'm Detective Webb and this is my partner Benson."

The two detectives were now going on their second straight shift and couldn't believe how busy they were before the weekend.

FIFTEEN

VUDU/KADEEM

Vudu was in the city of Milwaukee for only the second time in his adult life. His mother used to send him here from Chicago when he was a boy to spend summers with his dad's side of the family. But once he turned sixteen and thought he was too grown for his mother's rules, she let him be. Vudu started running the streets of the Windy City with the YG's, but he didn't sell drugs like the rest of his friends. Instead, he became J. Ross's personal hit man. Whenever they were together and the boss was upset, someone came up missing.

Folks learned quickly not to mess with the five foot seven monster after watching him kill a cop for turning off the fire hydrant on the kids as they played in it to cool off during one of the city's heat waves. The pressure to get jobs done by Ross, and a few others he did side jobs for, was not stressful to him. Vudu loved to kill ever since he was that boy who killed alley cats.

Billy was his first real body. They lived in the same project high-rise on different floors. One day Vudu caught Billy kissing a girl that he liked on the roof. He didn't make a scene. In fact, he didn't even let them know he was there. He waited until she went back inside the building. He then ran out and beat poor Billy with a pipe that he had found on the floor, and then tossed him off the sixteen-story building.

Now the treacherous killer was in Milwaukee to find and dispose of me and Gully because J. Ross believed we had set him up to get knocked. Vudu exited the highway on Highland Boulevard where he was told to start his search for us, knowing our clique was known as HPH, the Highland Park Hustlas. Vudu made a right heading northbound on 25th Street. He was in the heart of our hood. We aren't them fools down in the projects. Our hood is a residential area where we got money like the rest of them with less bullshit.

As he drove, he noticed a nice number of flashy cars and trucks—some old school, but most of them were new with big rims and custom paint jobs. As long as there wasn't snow on the ground, us Miltown boys were going to ride our big-boy toys. He figured this would be the best place to start looking for us.

A female walking with a young boy caught his eye. She looked good from behind with her shapely hips and ass like Buffy. He wondered if her hair was real or fake, but he still had to admit that it looked good flowing down her back. Vudu pulled over and parked half a block away from her, and then slid down in the seat so he wouldn't be noticed behind the tinted windows of his rented Jeep Compass.

Once the kid's school bus arrived, Vudu got out and followed the young woman, all the while checking out the alleys and abandoned houses. He was looking for a good spot to grab her, just as a truck pulled up and blew its horn at her. She quickly walked over to it and climbed inside as it then pulled off.

Vudu made his way back to the Jeep. He walked briskly, but not so much so that anyone would pay him any mind. By the time he stepped inside and drove in the direction he watched the big SUV turn, it was long gone.

"Damn!" he said out loud to himself as he punched the roof of the Jeep. "I bet that bitch knew where to find them niggas."

He pulled out a cigarette to smoke and calm his nerves as he rounded the block. That's when he came across two teenage boys with the same airbrushing on the back of their coats as the female he had followed earlier. He knew they weren't us, because he had seen us many times when we made the trip to re-up from Ross. But seeing them work off dope packs made him believe they could lead him to us. So he pulled up to the youngsters and tapped the horn to get their attention. When they raced toward him thinking they might have a sale, Vudu pulled out his gun and shot one of them point blank in the face, and the other boy twice in the side and back when he turned to run away.

Vudu then sped away until he was far enough away from the two warm bodies that he wouldn't be seen by any witnesses. But he parked close enough to see the action unfold. He watched as a squad car pulled up responding to a shot spotter only to find a murder scene. Vudu thought he might get lucky and see either one or both of us show up.

Ten minutes later his cell phone rang with the tone set for unknown callers.

"Who this?" he demanded when answering the call.

"What's good, fam? Tell me something."

"Oh shit, big homey," he responded, after recognizing the man's voice on the other end. "Did ya get out, or is this a three-way?"

"Yeah, I'm out. I'm just walking into the house. I had to pick up a new phone. Ya can't put shit past them Feds. Any progress on yo' end? Did you make it?"

"I'm here. I got a little something going on right as we speak, but I ain't seen neither of them bitch-ass niggas yet."

"Alright. Do what ya do. Hit me on this number. As a matter of fact, buy a new jack and hit me with the number as soon as you do," J. Ross ordered him before ending the call.

Vudu noticed the growing crowd around the scene of the shooting, but not the faces he was hoping for. After half an hour or so, the sky-blue Chrysler Aspen that picked up the woman he was following earlier pulled back up. He sat up in his seat so he could get a good look at the driver when he stepped out. But only two women got out—the girl from earlier and the driver. Almost an hour passed with no sign of us, his targets, so he decided to go to the mall to purchase a new phone and get something to eat before getting a room at one of the motels over on Wisconsin Avenue.

"What kinda niggas don't come check out what's going on in their hood where they getting their money at?" he asked himself, a habit he had picked up from spending so much time alone.

"That's this Milwaukee-ass shit for ya. I think I'ma go see Grandma," he decided, thinking it could save him some money if he had to stay the night.

Her house wasn't far from where he needed to be. She lived on 31st and Walnut, which was only a few blocks from Highland.

SIXTEEN

GP/CANDI

Candi couldn't believe everything had gone so wrong. She went from being a part of Calboy's family—a team player—to an ugly loner in a matter of hours. The beating she received from Annasta and her girlfriend hadn't worn off yet. Her face was still badly swollen and bruised. Candi knew she couldn't go back to Calboy looking the way she did and empty-handed after what she caused by not knowing that there was someone else in the apartment.

The bitch must think bro was Superman or somebody, because it never crossed her mind that telling Annasta where to find us was her death warrant alone.

Candi froze when she noticed someone stop right in front of the window of the motel where she had been hiding for over a week. She leaned over and peeked through the cracked curtain and saw what she thought was a woman trying to look inside. Candi started to get up just in case she had to defend herself. She sat back and relaxed when the woman moved on, but then someone started fooling with the doorknob.

Candi snatched up the gun she had taken when she broke

away from Marci after Annasta left them alone in B. Burns's apartment while she and her henchman went to confront Calboy about the robbery and shooting. Her survival instincts told her to aim for the door. But with her head still foggy from her misuse of prescription pills, she instead placed the gun in her lap. The door began to open by the time Candi remembered why she had picked up the gun and how to take the safety off.

"Candi! Candi!" her sister called out to her when she couldn't get past the chain on the door.

"I know you in there. Open the door. Let me in!"

"Yeah, yeah. I'm here," Candi's voiced slurred from the drugs.

"Well get yo' ass up and unhook the damn chain!"

Candi stuffed the gun under the pillow on the bed before she made her way to the door.

"How'd you get the door open?" she questioned after unlocking the door and opening it for her.

"I had the maid use her key. I told her I forgot mine and you were sleeping."

April hesitated when she got a look at her sister's face.

"What the fuck! Who did that to your face?" she demanded as she shut the door and locked it behind her.

"I got jumped by a couple of dyke bitches, but I don't wanna talk about it right now. Did Cal come looking for me at Momma's yet?"

"Oh shit, Candi. You don't know, do you?" April asked, taking a seat in the chair next to the door.

"Know what?" Candi dropped down on the bed facing her.

"Something happened. Calboy's dead," she said in a soft voice. "Somebody kicked in his door at his house and shot him and, I think, another girl. I'm here because GP and Wonda think you got something to do with it. Did you?"

"Fuck! I can't believe that bitch killed him!" Tears started falling from Candi's eyes. "April, you should go home, and don't come back here, because I won't be here.

"What! Oh my God, girl. You did have something to do with it, didn't you?"

"No, I didn't. I love him. I didn't know what she was gonna do to Calboy. I just wanted them to stop beating on me."

Candi's tears broke through the mental haze of the pills that she had taken.

"Get out, April! I wanna be by myself. Please don't tell nobody ya talked to me, and I won't be here if ya come back."

She held the door open for her sister to leave.

"Oh my God, Candi! Let me help you get through this. Ya

don't need to be by yourself right now. I won't tell nobody where you at, but I'm yo' sister. Don't shut me out. Please!"

"Just go. Ya don't know how much they all hate me. You can't help me, and I don't want you getting hurt because of me. And before ya say it, you know I can't go to the police."

Candi walked over to the bed and removed the gun from under the pillow.

"I'm good, April. I got me now. I'ma call you and let ya know I'm good when I make this right."

April realized that there was no more she could say to Candi, and she did not want to be in the same room with her and a gun in her emotional state of mind.

"You better. And be careful. I love you. Candi, you do have family ya can call on," she reminded her before making her exit, jogging back to her car, and speeding off.

Candi replaced all the locks on the door and wedged a chair against it for extra security. She then grabbed her purse, pulled out the bottle of pills and took four of them, and then washed them down with a flat grape soda. She then lay across the bed crying until the drugs took over and sent her to la-la land.

SEVENTEEN

KADEEM/GULLY

My partner navigated his custom Chrysler through the busy Windy City downtown nightlife, making his way back to the hotel with his captivating companion. I had recommended he make reservations way before he got there, so it wouldn't seem like a long-distance booty call since he liked Alima so much.

"Okay, ma. Is it okay if I ask you something personal?"

"Sure, that's what getting to know each other is about right?" Alima smiled. "Just don't bring up nothing that's going to dampen this good time I'm having with you."

"I don't wanna do that. So let me tell you it's about you, me, and your beliefs."

"My belief? By my belief, do you mean Islam? If that's it, then sure it's okay. I would actually like that."

"Okay. Well as ya know, my brotha is Muslim. Well, he likes to be called Islamic because of the life he's living in these streets and the way a lot of people make Muslims seem like the bad guys."

"I never thought of it that way, but I like the way he thinks.

I kinda wanted to ask you about it, but didn't want to run you off or make you think of me as anything other than me. So it's cool."

"Believe it or not, the day I met you, I told him that I think Islam is the reason I'm taken to you."

"Damn! I thought it was the way I looked in that outfit," she joked.

"It was that at first, but that's not what we talking about here."

Gully laughed along with her. He liked how easy it was talking to her.

"I want you to tell me about dating a woman like you, because I really wanna get to know ya better. Feel me?"

"Gully, you don't gotta look at me differently. Muslim or not, it's about respect. I'm single because a lot of men look at us women as less or like we're just here to serve them. When the truth is, Islam encourages you, meaning men, to treat us as equals. The Quran says the women's right over men is similar to those for men over women. Allah will hold us just as responsible for our actions as you and reward us accordingly. How does Kadeem treat the women he fools around with?"

"He don't have women; he just has one. He treats her like his queen from what I see. But his girl ain't Muslim. Well, she wasn't when they met anyway."

"And if he treats her the way ya say he does, then that means their relationship is doing fine. Do you think ours would be any different because we are the opposite of them?"

I don't know what to think.

A nigga just wanna know more of you.

I wanna explore you inside and out, and show ya what I'm about.

I'm more than thick and hung, I'm stout.

"And I can't think of nothing to go with that right now," Gully said while finishing his short rap.

"Okay. I was wondering where you were going with that. I see it's just yo' way of changing subjects."

"I never thought about it."

"When do I get to really hear what you can do? No, I wanna keep feeling special, so I'ma need you to write a song just for me."

"I can do that. Do a nigga got a time limit to have it done or what?" he asked, stopping in front of their destination.

"No. Take your time. I don't care for things that are rushed," she answered as the valet rushed over and opened the door for her.

"I plan on it."

Once they were inside the suite, Alima looked around because she had never been in a room as nice as it.

"Gully, how much was this room? You really didn't have to do this to impress me."

He filled two glasses with chilled champagne that was waiting for them in the room.

"What makes you think I got this room just for you? I like nice things too."

"You right. But from the things I've learned about you so far, I can't see you just chilling like this here."

She accepted the drink from him.

"Well, at the crib I don't need to, but since I'm in yo' city, I want us both to feel comfortable and safe."

He took a sip.

"And the price isn't for you to think about. The luxury of it is for ya to enjoy," he explained as he took hold of her free hand and led her over to the fireplace to sit.

"Hold on. Let me set the mood a little better then."

She turned on the radio, which filled the room with the soulful sound of Maxwell, before joining him by the fire.

"What station is this?" Gully asked surprised by the song.

"It's my phone. I plugged it into the radio," she explained.

They sat facing the big bay window overlooking the Great Lake that had a romantic full moon dancing for them across the water. Gully kicked off his shoes so he could wiggle his toes.

"Okay, Mr. Smooth, tell me why I deserve this treatment. Or do you just treat all yo' women this way on the first date?"

She flashed him a sexy smile before taking another sip of her drink.

"No, ma, this shit's new to me. It's new and different like you are to me. I don't know why ya won't believe a nigga when I tell ya all I do is work. The only bitch I make time for is my dog. So for me to go out like this here, ya gotta be special."

On that, she moved in and kissed him softly on the mouth.

"That's for you to think about until I come back from the bathroom."

Alima then got up and walked into the bathroom, where she decided to make use of the big tub and the time she had with Gully. She really wanted to see where things would go with him. But in the moment, all she could think about was having him inside of her, knowing she wouldn't be dissatisfied.

Gully heard the running water, and something about the sound of it sent a wave of excitement through his body. He was looking at the bathroom door, when Alima opened it wrapped only in a towel.

"Damn, ma!"

"Come here. I need your help with something."

She tossed her clothing his way piece by piece.

"Say no mo'."

He grabbed the bottle of champagne so they could finish it off in the tub or wherever. Once he followed her into the bathroom, he took off her towel, and she allowed him to have a good look at her almost flawless body.

"Do I get help with mine, or do I gotta do it myself?"

"No. Do it yourself. I like to watch. So make it sexy for me."

He did his best slow striptease. He first pulled off his shirt and let her get an eyeful of his muscular body. He flexed his big tatted arms and chest, and then seductively slid his hands down his firm abs on their way down to remove his pants. Then Gully walked over to her sitting in the water, bent down, and kissed her passionately before climbing in with her. He ran his hands up her leg, massaging his way between them. Alima grabbed him by his strong shoulders and tossed her head back moaning his name as his fingers worked like magic in and out of her. Gully's lips found her firm breasts, and he sucked and flicked her nipples. He then kissed her lips once more before diving down to replace his lips where his finger once was.

"Don't stop, baby! Yes, don't stop!" she cried out as she quaked and released. "Oooh! Stand up, baby."

He did as she asked and was blessed with her lips around his hardness as she inched it into her mouth until he felt her throat. Alima sucked him until his toes curled and he couldn't take it any longer.

"Don't hold back, baby! Let mama taste you."

She paused to encouraged him while continuing to stroke his length. When Gully busted, she milked him with her hands and then took him back into her warm mouth again, sucking him until he was nice and hard again.

Gully stood her up, turned her around, bent her over, and then worked his thickness deep inside of her wetness. Alima had to brace her hands against the wall as he plunged in and out of her repeatedly. He stroked even faster and harder, making her cum over and over until they almost fell out of the tub. Neither was finished with the other, so Gully scooped her in his arms and carried her back into the room to the bed with water still dripping from their bodies. They sexed like they had known each other a lot longer than they had. They took each other until they passed out.

EIGHTEEN

GP

It was late and I couldn't sleep, so I took a drive to clear my head. I kept thinking about Cal; and had I been paying more attention, he would still be here with me. My conscious was not letting me forget how much of a fuck-up I was. It kept flashing bro's face and reminding me of all the times we had together. I could even still hear the sound of his voice when I closed my eyes. I made my way back into the house and tried to sleep, but I still couldn't. The pain in my heart was so bad, all I could do was ball up like a baby and cry with old Smoke nestled beside me and giving me what comfort he could.

I must've fallen asleep, because the next time I looked up, it was light outside. I needed to get up, shower, and get dressed. When I was in the shower I decided to call Wonda and the girls. I knew that I needed to be around someone other than my cat.

"Hey, mama. I'm just checking to see if ya need anything?"

"I knew you would call one of these days, GP."

It hurt hearing how broken up she was.

"I wanna help you get that bitch. It's on you what we do to her. I just wanna be there when she's caught, so I can punch her in her shit. I need to break something on that hoe."

"Okay, Wonda. I understand, trust me! I ain't gonna stop ya from doing whatever to her. Hell, I was thinking last night that you might know more about the bitch than any of us anyway."

"Yeah. I already talked to Lyte about it."

"I bet ya did. What she say?" I asked, pouring Smoke a bit of milk in his dish.

"She's with it, with or without us. Roc may never walk again because of that punk bitch. Lyte gotta do for him and the baby by herself."

"No, never that! I won't let her do it all on her own. Bro put us together for a reason—to get money as a unit as a family, and that's what we gonna stay as," I reminded her.

"I know, I know. It's just that my head is just so fucked up right now, that's all."

I spent the next half hour talking to her and found out a lot about Candi. Wonda had phone numbers to a few of Candi's family members, whom Wonda had already called, and was told that they hadn't seen or heard from her in weeks. I wonderde where this hoe up and disappeared to. Before ending the call so I could rush to class, I promised Wonda I would be over there afterward.

~ ~ ~

Apple took a deep breath trying to gather her thoughts. Her mind was all over the place and had her feeling all empty inside. She turned on her cell phone's camcorder and stationed it so she could leave us her goodbye. When Apple looked at her reflection in the mirror on the dresser as she passed by, she saw that she had lost weight. Her eyes were bloodshot from all the crying and fatigue. She almost looked like a zombie instead of a grieving lover and friend.

"I don't know how to start this. All I keep seeing is Calboy getting shot. He was killed trying to save me. I—I can remember the look on his face when the bullets hit him and the sound of his body slamming to the floor."

She shook her head trying to get rid of the memory.

"I'm not crazy! I'm not. He was just—just the best thing that ever happened to me. He showed me that I was more than just his hoe or his money maker. I know I was, because daddy not only told me, but he showed me when he gave his life for mine."

Tears began to fall harder, and so did the snow outside her bedroom window.

Apple dropped her eyes to the Glock 23 that she held in her lap. She didn't know if it was visible or not to the camera, and she really didn't care if it was at this point. All Apple kept telling herself was that she couldn't live and that she didn't want to live without Calboy. The sudden knock at the door startled her, which caused her to jump to her feet with the gun firmly in her unsteady hands.

Looking out the opening in her curtain, she could see my car.

"What? Go away!"

"Open the damn door, Apple! You've been cooped up in there for too damn long!" I yelled through the door. "Come out here and talk to us. Wonda's cooking. She told me ya ain't been eating. Girl, open this door. We need to be together right now. Come eat with us. This ain't the time to be alone. We need to stay together as a family like bro always told us. We all we got."

The first thing I saw when she opened the door was her bloodshot eyes and then the gun at her side.

"Apple, what ya about to do with that?"

I forced the door all the way open and held out my hand.

"Give me that damn gun, Apple!"

She hesitated at first, but then she saw I wasn't backing down and I wasn't giving up on her. When she gave it to me, she broke down crying hard. I held her in my arms to keep her from falling to the floor. Wonda appeared at my call and took the gun out of my hand, just in case Apple decided to continue with her first plan and maybe try to take me with her.

"We miss him too. I miss him so much, just like you do. I felt lost until Cal came into my life. He gave me a home and all y'all to be my family," Wonda told her as she joined in on the hug.

"Ma, he died because of me! I should've looked before I opened the door."

"No! Stop that! It's not yours or any one of our faults. Candi's bitch-ass did this to us. She's the one to blame for bro and Rocky. That shit was her doing. The bitch had to be the one to tell them niggas where to find us."

I looked into Apple's eyes and made her a promise.

"I'ma kill that bitch when we catch her."

"And we need you, Apple. We gotta pull together like GP told me. We still a family. Come on, girl! Get in this bathroom and let me help you get yourself together," Creamy said to her while pulling her toward the bathroom.

"Gale, thanks for coming. We been trying to get her outta that room for days."

"Wonda, ya don't gotta thank me. We supposed to be there for each other."

I hugged her.

"We all we got, right?"

"Yeah! All we got with bro looking over us. And for that reason, there's no love for that bum bitch. I'ma beat her ass and then empty this clip right into her face," I said while reaching for the gun.

"I want the bitch to have a closed casket."

Wonda handed me back the gun.

"Come help me get this food together. Let's eat and talk about what to do next."

On the way to the kitchen, I stopped and peeked into the bathroom to check on Apple. Creamy had stripped her out of her dirty clothes and put her in the shower. She was picking the clothes up off the floor to put them in the hamper when she saw me.

"How she doing?"

"She gonna be okay. She just needed us and a kick in the ass to get her mind right."

We heard Apple laugh.

"What you laughing at, hoe? Ya know I'll put the smackdown if either Wonda or GP tell me to."

"And that'll be the day the world stops spinning," she responded, peeking her head out from the shower.

"Now that's the bitch I know right there. Now hurry yo' ass up. Wonda's trying to make me help her cook and shit."

I smiled at her and then left them to see what Wonda needed my help with in the kitchen.

NINETEEN

KADEEM/J. ROSS

J Ross sat behind his gorgeously polished chrome-and-dark marble desk inside his office located in his two-story family home in Elgin, Illinois. The home had seven bedrooms and an open vestibule off the kitchen that led to the office and master bedroom. Right now his family wasn't there. His wife was a short Nigerian and British light-skinned bella who often took their two daughters out shopping as a distraction. Their house was being decorated for the surprise birthday party he was giving his girls early because he was due in court on the day of their actual day.

It was halftime during the Bears and Packers game that he was watching on the 50-inch ultra-thin television hanging on the wall. The game made him think about me and Gully and revisit the day of his arrest, so he picked up one of his four phones and called his very well-paid lawyer, a man named Greg Long.

"Mr. Ross, I was just thinking of calling you," he answered on the third ring.

"I bet you were."

"No, it's true. I already know what you're calling about."

"Okay, Mr. Mind Reader, get to it. What's your progress?" J. Ross asked as he remotely unlocked the door for his personal assistant, Sonya, after being alerted by the security system that showed her on the television screen.

"Mr. Ross, I'm not going to BS you like what I got to say is good news. All I was able to do was get a copy of a redacted file on you, but I'm still working on getting the open file."

"I would expect so. But tell me, did you get anything from the one you have now?"

"Hey, Jay, you want me to refill your drink?" Sonya asked when she entered the office and saw her boss on the phone.

He answered with a nod, and she refilled his glass as well as poured one for herself.

"All this file tells me is that you had some dealings with this person numerous times. Tell me, do you know anyone who works on the docks and the ballpark?"

"Shit, Greg! That could be anybody. I was at both of those places just before the Feds kicked in the door. Man, get me something I can use! I need names."

"I'm working on doing just that. Sir, whomever this is, I do believe they're close to you."

"Greg, ya should've started with that. But okay, I'm

paying you to find out who it is and make it go away. So do your job and get me what I need."

"I'm on it, sir."

J. Ross ended the call without another word. The news the lawyer did have made Ross question his hasty order given to Vudu without knowing who the rat truly was. Ross knew we didn't know about his dealings on the docks. But that didn't help him with his issues because there were so many that did. All he knew was whoever got in his way would die, and he didn't have a problem with that.

What Long said posed a serious threat to J. Ross's freedom and his family's way of life. To him, that was reason enough not to tell Vudu to stand down. But he still wondered if it was the right precaution. His instincts were right most of the time, and right now they told him that he was missing something.

"I need you to keep an eye on Ed," he announced, now looking from the TV to Sonya. "He likes you, so use that to get in, and report back to me on the moves that nigga makes."

"Why the mistrust all of a sudden?" she questioned, hating the job of babysitting that Ross was ordering her to do.

But she wouldn't complain. Sonya just waited for him to give her the green light to do what she loved to do. Sonya thought that by working for the kingpin, she would've been allowed to kill more people, but all she was so far was J. Ross's permanent side chick.

"The lawyer thinks the rat is someone close to me, and the two closest to me are Ed and you."

"Well, I'm glad you know my loyalty is to you—and you only!" she reminded him, before slamming down the rest of her drink.

"How long will it be before Renee and the girls get back?" she asked, slipping out of her gun and Hurt shirt.

"They went shopping for the party."

He watched her undress.

"Then you got time to put me in the mood to deal with that fat fuck."

Sonya dropped down between his legs and set his hardness free.

"I don't give a fuck what you say, but I'm not letting him put his little dirty dick in me. This poo-poo is only for you."

"Now, baby, you gotta make him think it's real. So don't be that way. I know what's mine. You don't gotta worry about that."

"Well, I hope the fat boy can work his tongue good, because it's gonna take a lot of work to play this role."

She smiled and then slid down on his thickness, loving

every inch of it as he forced it deeper inside her.

~ ~ ~

Detective Rodgers hung on every word as two officers from his surveillance team reported in after following Big Ed.

"Our man just pulled up to the house now. He has an unknown female with him, and they're going inside now. I believe our man is armed."

"Which man?"

"Oh, sorry, sir. Ed, I believe he put a gun in his waste."

"Ben, are you sure you saw a gun?"

"Not really. It's kinda hard to see from where we are parked. But if I would guess, I'd say it's a big black revolver— maybe a .357 or .44."

Rodgers turned to Dickerson, who was eyeing a couple of hookers working the strip.

"Ben thinks old Ed is carrying. What do you want to do?"

"Just sit tight and stay awake. I need him to be using the gun to commit a real crime like murder. Tell them to keep us posted."

Rodgers told the men to just keep their eyes open.

"I want these assholes under the prison, and a petty gun

charge ain't gonna do it!"

Dickerson then got out of the van to go talk to the hookers.

Rodgers couldn't believe his partner was thinking with his little head instead of his big one right now. He felt that something must be up for Big Ed to be carrying a gun. J. Ross's high-powered lawyer pulled some major strings to get them out on bail, so why fuck that up by carrying? Did he fear for his life because the two hadn't been seen much together since posting bail? This was what was running through Rodgers' head while his partner was off in some alley getting some head. The detective picked up his phone and called Dickerson.

"What is it that couldn't wait?"

"Don't you think it's funny that Big Ed hardly talked to his lady friend on the drive?"

"No, not really. Hey, buddy, let's finish this conversation when I'm done with this interview."

"Asshole!" he said out loud after Dickerson hung up on him.

He called the fifth man in his team, Geoff.

"Yeah, boss?" Geoff answered on the first ring.

"Was you able to get inside Big Ed's place?"

"Yes, I'm bugging it now. Do we still have eyes on him,

because I don't want to get caught in here by that big son of a bitch."

"Yeah we do, but work fast and get out of there. And don't leave a mess!"

"Hey, hey! I got this!" Geoff ended the call to get back to work.

Just to keep busy, Detective Rodgers got out his laptop and pulled up Big Ed and J. Ross's case file to try to see what he was missing. He had a hunch that Ed knew his car was bugged and that's why he didn't say much to his date in the car. He got to thinking that the unknown female wasn't just some random chick he picked up to get his rocks off.

On that thought, he saw his partner strolling back toward the van and openly drinking on the job.

"If he blows this for me, I'm going to kill him!" Rodgers said, exasperated with his partner's conduct since they caught this case.

TWENTY

GP

Cal's funeral looked more like a car show than anything. All the well-known and unknown hustlers and pimps came out to say goodbye to one of their fallen. Pastor Blake gave his best speech and reminded us of the good Lord's instructions. He only highlighted the good that Calboy had done in his life. At times, I didn't know if I was at the right place because of some of the things that the pastor was saying. But before the beautiful honey pine-and-brass casket was lowered into the dark cold ground, I was deep in tears again.

I stopped the recording and turned off the television, letting the dark envelope me until I got my heartbroken prayer out. I couldn't stand this shit any longer. It'd been weeks since the funeral. Bro wouldn't want me feeling sad and sitting at home alone with my cat.

I tried to bury myself in my schooling, but found I couldn't stay focused. So I asked the teachers to give me what I needed, so I wouldn't fall far behind and take a break from it. But in just a few days, I had done all the work and was in need of something to do before I did something stupid. I don't mean like Apple, but like going over to that bitch mom's crib and beating her until she became clairvoyant or some shit. I couldn't believe how good that bitch Candi was doing at staying low. I guess she wasn't as dumb as I thought.

I rolled out of bed, turned on the light, and walked into the closet. I was almost moving on autopilot. I moved a few boxes out of the way so I could get to and open the small secret door on the lower far wall. I pulled out a dark green duffel bag. Calboy used to call this my to-go bag, because it had everything I needed to get outta town fast if or when the time came. A bitch knows she can't keep living the life I live forever. Everybody's luck runs out. So I kept two fake IDs, ten G's in cash, two guns, a change of clothes, and a prepaid phone ready at all times. But this wasn't what I wanted, so I reached back into the space and removed the wooden chest that held my guns. Two Heckler & Koch 45s, two Glock 19s, two Glock 23s, and two small assault rifles, all from a gun store we hit a few years back. I didn't need anything big for what I had in mind, so the Glock 19 would do. I had the one I wanted and put everything back the way it was before looking for an outfit to wear out to the casino.

After about fifteen minutes or so I decided on a coffee-and-tan-sequined top and denim overalls by True Religion, brown soft-leather boots by Aldo, and a knitted soft-leather bag by Lucky Brand to carry my gun and other necessities. I laid it all out on the bed and then called both Wonda and Apple on a three-way line and told them to get dressed.

"Get dressed how and for what?" Wonda asked.

"I'm already dressed unless ya need a bitch to suit up for some action."

"That's exactly what I need y'all dressed for, Apple. We going out to the casino to get drunk and have fun—in that order. I'm already getting my shit on, so no is not an option."

All Wonda and Apple did was mope around the house missing bro. They knew he was far from the perfect man in their lives, but he did love them, and they missed that love. Wonda told me she felt lonely inside without him. She loved the smell of his pillows that still held his place in her bed. Apple also felt that loneliness, only hers was laced with anger. She hated herself for not being the girl on the inside of the apartment that night. She knew Calboy would be pushing her to go out with me, so she could come up on some new clients or their next robbery, the way Creamy was out doing right now.

Both of my girls agreed to go out with me and went to work putting themselves together. In bro's memory, Wonda decided to drive his honey-gold-colored Audi A8 sitting on 24-inch black-and-gold Diablo rims for their night out on the town. After picking me up, the three of us floated down to the busy casino, valeted the car for safe keeping, and went inside.

~ ~ ~

The freshly washed and waxed Chrysler Aspen sparkled as it pulled into the closest available parking slot. Its three occupants exited the lower level of the garage, crossed the street, and entered the lobby of the casino not long after we did. Like us, they were enticed by the cheering from the hot crap tables and slots. They all came with a nice sum of cash and prayed to leave with more; if not, then have a good time losing most of it.

Kadeem felt the need to warm up a bit before he got on the craps table, so he told KC and Gully he would catch up with them at the tables. He then made his way to a crowded roulette wheel, where he squeezed in next to us. He displayed a nice-sized wad of cash that caught all of our attention, peeled off $200 and got a stack of chips. He put five chips down on 9 and watched the wheel spin, with the ball bouncing wildly over number after number until it landed on 5. Not giving up, Wood repeated his bet and called a waitress over to take his drink order. An older woman on the other side of him told him that he should spread his bets, so he took her advice and let the wheel spin.

Gully broke away from KC to get in on the poker table, leaving him at the slots playing Jackpot Party. Gully slid in between two men at the table that looked to be having a good run. The seasoned thug checked faces around the table to see if he knew any of the players. When he didn't recognize anyone, he bought into the game and quickly lost $500. He wasn't feeling the way they were playing the game at the table, so he moved to the craps table where he felt his luck would be better.

As Gully approached, Wonda's ass caught his eye. He saw that she was a tall, thick, dark-skinned beauty. He liked the way her Juicy Couture catsuit hugged her full curves, so he eased up next to her so he could get a closer look and try to get to know her.

"Say, ma, I see ya seem to know what to do with them dice. How about we work together and strip these lames?"

"I'm doing just fine on my own, and I don't know if you can play or more yet pay yo' way," she answered, showing him her dimples.

"I can show ya better. I know that actions speak louder."

He bought in the game with $1,000 to match what he thought he counted in Wonda's stacks of chips.

"Why don't you place the bet and watch me work?"

"Okay. How much?"

"Whatever ya want. I gotta show ya I know what I'm doing, and that I can afford to play in yo' game, right?"

"Okay, show off then."

She pushed over half of his chips on 8.

"This is one of my lucky numbers."

"One of yo' lucky numbers. How many do you got?" he joked.

"I see ya left us drinking money, so let me get a Hen and your name. You can get whatever ya want," he told her before he then tossed the dice, landing on her number.

Wonda was impressed.

"Juicy."

"What?"

"My name is Juicy. Now what's yours?" she asked while flagging down the waitress.

"Gully. Juicy, huh? I wonder why they call you that?"

"I'm sure ya seen why before you came over here."

She smiled and then turned so he could see her butt while

she gave the drink order to the waitress.

"Let me get a beer with that too."

Before long, all the hooting and cheering at the table was for them. All the excitement made us come over to watch the show along with Gully's friends. When Wonda saw us, she pulled us away from her new friend and told us the name she was using so we wouldn't expose her true name.

"Shit, that's what I'm talking about. Do yo' thang, Ms. Juicy."

While I cheered her on, Wonda was wondering if it was too soon to be doing what she was thinking of doing with Gully. Not because she just met him. She was a whore when she met Calboy, so the one-night-stand thing was nothing to her. It was that she buried her man. After a few more drinks, Juicy made up her mind and decided to give Gully the fuck of his life.

"Here, Apple. Take the car home. I'ma text y'all and let you know where I'm at and the kinda car he's driving."

She then handed her the keys.

"Mama, I'ma need that plate number too. So send me a picture of it," Apple told her.

I turned on the Friend Finder app on our phones.

"Wonda, ya want my baby to be safe?"

"GP, I don't think we are going to be doing nothing that has to do with me needing a gun. Anyway, as long as I know y'all on point, I'm good," Juicy said as she turned the offer down.

Gully told his guys that he was getting a room there with Juicy, and they wished him luck and decided to call it a night as well. They called for a car to take them home. Before the car got there, KC's girl was there to pick him up in his car to make sure he came home to her. So he dropped off Kadeem at home, not wanting to leave him to have to take a cab.

As for me and Apple, the night was still young, and neither of us was ready for it to end. Apple felt like dancing, so we decided on hitting the south-side club scene. We ended up at Club Trix, where the crowd was mixed and jumping. We fit right in drinking and doing our thang on the dance floor. I noticed how much Apple was grinding up on me and pushing all others away who wanted to get in on our dance. It wasn't a secret that Apple was bisexual. She called it being free to love who you loved and how ya wanted to. What she didn't know was I was feeling kinda curious. There were many nights I would get caught up in the girls telling stories about how many women paid to spend time with them just like the men did. But I had never been with a female.

I'm sure she was only feeling me because I was as strong-minded as Cal and very independent. The opposite of her. Apple knew she couldn't make it on her own. None of them could. Without exchanging words, I knew they were all looking for me to be the new leader. We left when the DJ announced last call over the sound system. I drove since I wasn't going to trust our lives in Apple's wasted hands. I drove back to my place because I didn't want Apple in that house alone, not after her suicide attempt. With Creamy hard at work somewhere and Wonda—a.k.a. Juicy—getting her back broke by some random guy she had fun shooting dice with, I knew it was best for her to stay with me until one of them called.

As soon as we got inside, Smoke ran up to me while Apple rushed to the bathroom. I made my way into the kitchen to get us some napkins, because they had forgotten to give us some with the food we stopped to get on the way home. I then went into my bedroom to get out of my club clothes so I could go right to bed after I ate. That's when Apple came staggering into the room naked from the waist up and carrying her form-fitting dress in her hands.

"Girl, I see ya feeling good. Here, drink this."

I handed her a glass of water and then watched her lie

across the bed before I went into the bathroom.

I couldn't shake the arousal I had for her, so I decided to take a quick shower. Before tonight I had never looked at her or any of them in this way, but there was something in the air. Our lives were different now, and thinking of Apple lying half naked in my bed made me turn on the cold water to calm my lust.

I was exhausted after the shower and knew Apple had to be as well. Maybe she had fallen asleep. I hope she did anyway. And she was. Apple's drunk ass was passed out in the same spot I left her on the bed snoring softly. I walked on the other side of the bed, dropped my towel, and sat down. A few moments went by before I felt her hand sliding around my hip and then rubbing between my thighs. I took hold of her hand, pausing the hot sensation her fingers were causing. When I turned back to face Apple, her eyes were wide open.

"Don't stop me, GP. Just lay with me right now, please?"

"Take yo' drunk ass to sleep, Apple."

"Lay down with me."

She pulled me down to her and kissed me.

I had never kissed a girl before, but didn't stop it. Her hand found my breasts and my nipples hard. Fuck it! Why not do this with her, I thought as I pulled her closer to match her passion. I was shaking my wetness and twitched, which sent waves of heat through my body as she flipped me onto my back and got down between my legs. Then I felt her fingers part me and her tongue on my clit. I moaned and purred. Before I knew it, I had one hand in her hair and the other digging into my thigh from the way she was eating my kitty. I didn't even try to fight the orgasm that she pulled out of me. She was so hot and sexy that I pulled her up so I could taste my cum on her lips.

She pushed down and straddled my right thigh, grinding and humping her wetness on me and trying to get herself off. I flipped her over and took her hard nipple in my mouth, sucking and licking until I heard her purring and pushing me down. Once I was between her big thighs, I repeated what she did to me. Only I let my fingers dance in her and kissed her starting from her knee up until my warm mouth was on her mound and my tongue on her clit, the way hers was on mine moments ago. Apple came hard, letting me know I was doing my thang on her. When she was done, she pulled me up for a kiss and we molded into each other like two confident lovers. I knew this was crossing the line between friends, but it was too late now. I'd blame it on being drunk in if things were awkward in the morning.

TWENTY-ONE

KADEEM/VUDU

Vudu woke up at about 9:30 p.m. For just a moment he thought back to when he was a kid and how his grandma would wake him and his cousins up with a hot breakfast. He loved the smell of bacon and eggs in the air. If he was at home right now, he would be making a high protein shake to slam down before doing his calisthenics. The voices he heard in the kitchen didn't belong to his grandma, and he knew just who they were by the sound of their laughter. It was his cousins Bay and Jazz.

"What y'all fools burning up in here?" he asked while walking into the kitchen where they were.

"Now, nigga, ya know I don't fuck up no bacon. I might not cook shit else, but I'm the truth with breakfast food and all things microwaveable," Bay reminded him while looking up from the stove.

"What it do, cuzo? I know you not up here because ya miss us, so put us in. I know how you get down, Vu. Let us help so we can put a lil' cash in our pockets."

"Jazz, keep that down. I don't want grandma to hear that

shit."

"Nigga, she at bingo, and she knows yo' ass up to something too."

"Why do ya think we over here? She told us to come help you so you won't get popped off 'cause yo' ass don't know yo' way around no mo'. So ya stuck with us, cuzo."

Vudu knew he could use their help in finding us, so he filled them in on the reason he was up the Mil.

"I can only give y'all like two G's right now and hit ya with something else when it's done, okay?"

"Shit! I'm cool with that. That's a G each, and we get to keep whatever we strip off them niggas. Deal!" Bay told him excitedly.

Vudu couldn't believe how easy it was to get them online with him, and he saved some money because they misunderstood his offer when he told them that he was going to pay them two G's—which he meant for each of them.

~ ~ ~

That was over two weeks ago, and day in, day out since, the three stone-hearted assassins circled the Highland Park area looking for their prey. But they quickly found out that we weren't that easy to find. Vudu noticed his cousins were getting restless. So he thought a break was needed if he didn't want to lose the only help he had.

"Hey, let's go check out that strip joint we keep passing over on State Street for a minute. Then we can jet back over here and sit on the studio," he suggested.

"Sounds like a plan to me. I'm always down to look at some half-naked bitches," Jazz said as he passed the blunt over to Vudu.

"Vu, ya might run into an old girl ya met at the store the other day," Bay told him, turning the jeep around to head to Ricky's Gentlemen's Club. "Did ya even call the bitch yet?"

"Nope! I ain't had the time. But why you say I'ma run into her there. What ya know that I don't?"

"Fam, ya don't listen, do you? The bitch said she was on her way to work at the club, and that's the only muthafuckin' one over there, right?"

"You act like I should know that shit. I don't live in this janky-ass city like you. All I was concerned with was that ass in them jeans and putting the boy in her mouth. But since ya said it, I'ma call her now and see if she at work, so I can put my bid in for a shot of that ass later. I ain't got in-house pussy like you niggas do."

Vudu decided to text her instead, knowing if she was in the club, she wouldn't be able to talk.

They found a place to park so they could make a quick getaway if they needed to. Vudu checked his phone to see if Candi had answered his text as they waited in line outside of the entrance of Ricky's. As always, everything was on him. He paid the bouncer the cover charge for all of them, submitted to the pat-down, and then entered the club. Inside they were shown to their table by a big-boobed white girl with pink hair, dressed in a transparent, short, lacy, tight dress.

"Please don't bite my head off, but it's just my job to remind you guys of the two-drink minimum—and soda don't count. But I can see it ain't nothing to you bosses." She gave them her best smile and sales pitch. "Let me know when y'all ready to order."

"We ready now. Do y'all got bottle service here, or is it just by the glass?" Vudu asked as he surveyed his surroundings and the butt of a short Latina in a red-and-black leather negligee and thigh-high boots.

"Of course we do. What would you like?"

"Two Rose, Hennessy, and a pitcher of MGD. And some hot skins, if ya got 'em."

"Do that take care of the two-drink shit you told us about?

If not, come back so a nigga can buy you a drink or two," Jazz flirted with her.

"Yes, you're covered, daddy, but you can still buy me that drink, or just buy me." She smiled, winking her long eyelashes at him. "A new girl will be onstage in a few, but you can go enjoy any of the girls on the other two stages."

She then pointed them toward the other smaller stages where two girls were putting in the work.

"Hold up before ya go. Do you know if Candi is working tonight?" Vudu asked.

"Yeah, she's always here. I believe she's the one up next on the main stage. In case I didn't tell you, my name is Pink," she introduced herself, looking Jazz in the eyes.

The next girl strutted onto the stage next to them.

"I'll be back with your drinks shortly. In the meantime, enjoy my girl Taboo," she encouraged them, before she rushed off to fill their drink orders.

Vudu continued to scan the club hoping to spot one or both of us. Business seemed to be good in the strip club. All the girls were busy dancing onstage or giving lap dances in just about every corner he looked.

"Oh, so you can't call me, but ya can come look up my ass?" Candi asked when she stopped at Vudu's table.

She stood with her hands on her hips pretending to be upset with him.

"Say, say. Don't be like that. A nigga texted you, and when ya didn't hit me back, I came looking for you. And, yes, I wanna see that ass in action," he explained, holding out his hand to her.

"When I'm done with my set, I'ma check my phone and see if ya lying to me. If you are, in here is gonna be the only way you gonna see this ass."

She slapped his hand away and then smiled as she turned to leave.

"Hey, hold up, ma. What do I get if I'm not?"

"Nigga, what ya think? You get a bad bitch on yo' side!" Candi answered before she then rushed off to take her place on the main stage.

~ ~ ~

Ms. Luscious couldn't get her cash off the runway fast enough before the lights started changing colors and flashing actively to the beat of Nelly's hit song "Tip Drill" and the DJ announcing the spectacular act to the stage. A dancer with a body like Blac Chyna dressed in cut-off, form-fitting jean shorts and fishnet stockings charged through the beaded curtain. She immediately mesmerized all the men and women around. Many got up from their seats to get a better view of how she worked her body, and there was no issue quickly making it rain all sized bills on her and littering the stage.

"Annasta, did you like my dance?" Ms. Luscious asked, side-stepping a few men who tipped small just to cop a feel.

"Baby girl, ya know how I do. Like it or not, I need to find out if you can do all that tricky shit on this dick."

"Well it ain't hard for you to find out first-hand what my luscious can do," she flirted while twirling her wide hips hoping to tempt Annasta into a date.

Ms. Luscious moved closer to her.

"Ain't you gonna tip me, or do ya wanna go for a one-on-one?"

"Bitch! Tip yo' fool ass out my daddy face unless you trying to be down and break bread, hoe," Marci challenged, suddenly materializing behind them and pushing past Ms. Luscious to sit on Annasta's lap.

"You heard her, so now ya got a choice to make. Leave now or pay me, bitch!" Annasta told her and then downed a shot of Patron.

Ms. Luscious backed down and rolled her eyes at Marci before stomping away. Annasta's eyes followed her bouncing butt until Ms. Luscious found someone's lap to bounce it in. Then Annasta turned her lustful eyes to the dancer onstage. She was enjoying the way the girl worked the pole, and wished Marci wasn't around so she could maybe get to know the girl dancing one night.

Marci noticed the way Annasta was gazing at the girl on the stage and knew that if she didn't intervene now, this could be a problem for her in the future.

"Do you want that one for tonight, daddy? I can get her to leave with us, because I know the bitch wants me," she lied, knowing Creamy hadn't looked her way once since they had been working together.

It has been awhile since we had a plaything.

"So, yeah, baby, if ya can get her, let's have some fun with that tonight. Do you know if she's under orders, because I don't wanna have to fuck a nigga up."

"Noooo! I don't think so, because I've never seen her with a nigga that wasn't a regular here. But I'll find out."

"Do that and then toss some cash her way and bring her to the spot. After I fuck the living hell outta the bitch, she gonna give my shit back and some of hers begging for round two."

Annasta nudged Marci on her way to do as she was told at the end of Creamy's sets.

Marci followed Creamy into the dressing room to take a break before getting changed for her next set.

"Bitch you did yo' thang out there just now. You gotta teach me how to work that brass dick the way you do. Creamy got 'em going crazy!" she said as she sat down across from her.

"I ain't gotta problem with that. I can show ya a few of my tricks before the club gets busy one of these days. Just not after, 'cause I keep my money on live like all always," she answered while stepping into a pair of gold-tipped stiletto boots and then zipping them up.

"You on! Here, let me help you with that."

Marci took hold of her foot and caressed Creamy's strong calf as she zipped the boot up for her.

"Do ya got a full plate tonight? If you got room for two more, Annasta told me to make it worth your while if ya do. So let's start with $100 and work from there?"

Marci knew if she told her that she was with a baller, it would make her believe she could get cashed out for the time she spent with them.

Creamy couldn't believe that Marci had just put one of the main suspects in Calboy's murder—the dyke sister—in her hands. She didn't want to let on that that she knew the connection or let them know hers.

"If Annasta or whatever ya call him ain't coming off $200-$400 for couples to start, then he can't afford me."

She stood up and checked herself over in the full-length mirror.

"Creamy, that ain't shit! I can put that in yo' hand right now. Ya must don't know who my daddy is, do you?"

"Oh, I don't do pimps, so I'll pass. I got all I need at home."

"I promise you it ain't like that. We just trying to have fun. I'll give ya a stack for the rest of the night. Half now and the rest when ya get there," Marci pledged, not wanting to let Annasta down.

"Hey! When money talks, I'm open!"

Creamy held out her hand for the cash that Marci had promised. Little did Marci know, she would've done it for free just to find out what she could about the whereabouts of B. Burns and Candi.

Marci went over to her locker and got the money.

"Now be ready when the club closes, and I'm riding with you just in case ya get on a change of heart with my money," she told her while holding out the wad of cash to her.

"You know, you seem cool! So hold onto that until I see

what's up with the date I got set up already. He's one of my reggies, and I don't want to lose him. I know ya know what I'm talking about, so let me holla at him out here. Afterward, I'll follow y'all where we gotta go."

"Okay, that sounds like a plan."

Marci leaned in and kissed her on the corner of her mouth, and then went off to tell Annasta the good news.

TWENTY-TWO

GP

Almost every day since Lyte was able to bring Roc home from the hospital, she had been struggling to take care of him on her own. Many of the customers that Roc had on his line for weed jumped ship on him now that he was a paraplegic, specifically the ones he fronted it to. Because of his condition, Roc wouldn't let Lyte ask any of us for help or allow anyone besides his sister over to their house. Needless to say, he was embarrassed about being paralyzed, and his depression ran deep, hitting him from all sides hard.

It was so much so that Lyte didn't like leaving him alone, but she had a much-needed doctor's appointment today to check on the progress of their unborn child. The possibility of being in a wheelchair for the rest of his life not only had Roc depressed, but also very insecure of her love for him and jealous of any man that looked her way. So to ease his mind, she asked his sister, Tanika, to go with her to the appointment and leave him alone.

Lyte missed us dearly. Even though I checked in on them by text and the others hit them up on Facebook, she needed to hear the sound of our voices. She couldn't call us around Roc without him going into a fit, so she used the little time she had away now to get up with us on the phone. Our girl needed a break and some encouraging words from her friends before she went crazy trying to care for the man she loved.

~ ~ ~

The sound of the shower woke Juicy up. Her eyes had to get used to the strange darkness because she was used to the morning sun pouring in through her bedroom curtains. She instinctively reached for the lamp on the nightstand and found it wasn't there. That's when Juicy remembered she didn't go home the night before. And the sweet pains that shot throughout her body from the workout that was put on her the night before reminded her whom she was with at the hotel.

As quietly as she could, Juicy got out of the bed and collected her things so she could creep out of the room while Gully was in the shower. But when she saw his silhouette through the frosted steamy shower glass, she decided to go in for another round to top off her one-night stand.

When she opened the door to the shower, Gully turned to find Juicy standing there naked.

"Did I wake you up?"

"No, not really. I'm a morning person anyway." Her eyes dropped to his sleeping manhood. "Is there room for two?"

Before he could answer, she stepped inside and instantaneously dipped down to take him into her soft full lips. She sucked him until he was nice and hard, and then she stood up. Gully lustfully spun her around, and Juicy eagerly bent over to allow him to slide deep inside her from behind. Gully was hitting it just the way she needed him to—nice and hard. In fact, it was so hard that she had to brace herself against the shower wall with both hands. But she was loving every minute of it. Juicy heard her cell phone ringing a familiar ringtone, but she wasn't going to stop him until she got what she needed.

~ ~ ~

"Oh, so yo' fat ass can call GP but nobody else, huh?" Apple asked Lyte while answering the phone.

"Fuck you, bitch! I ain't fat. It's called a baby!" Lyte laughed. "It ain't like that. I only called her because Wonda didn't answer her phone. Apple, why ya got GP's phone? Where y'all bitches at?"

"Well, GP made us go out with her last night and shit. We

got fucked up. Wonda found her some dick to put in her mouth, and Creamy should have her ass at the house asleep. Ya know that's all that bitch do when she's working. I'm making breakfast for me and GP."

"You're making breakfast? Don't tell me you finally got what ya wanted with yo' freaky ass?"

"Yeah, but shut up, tramp. I don't know how she's gonna feel about y'all knowing about it yet."

"Oh, okay. Where she at now?"

"She's in the bathroom somewhere. I don't know. I'm in the kitchen with her jealous-ass cat. Is everything alright with them two over there?" GP asked while walking into the kitchen, scooping up Smoke and smoking a blunt.

"I don't know. We ain't got that far yet. Her nosey butt ain't stopped asking me shit long enough for me to ask her."

"Put her on speaker so I can holla at her too."

"Don't try to do me, Apple! Yo' ass was just as eager to answer me."

They all laughed.

"You sound like you outside. Where's bro?" she asked while setting Smoke on the counter so she could get him something to eat.

"I'm on my way to the doctor for the baby's checkup.

Roc's at the house all by himself today."

"Why's Tanika ain't with him, or is he doing better?"

"No, not too much."

We could hear Lyte's sadness.

"I asked Tanika to come with me to this appointment so he won't think I'm out cheating or trying to leave him."

"No! It ain't that bad, is it?" Apple asked, fixing our plates with cheese eggs, chop steak, and buttermilk toast.

"Girl, y'all don't know the hell I'm in. Roc be tripping if I meet the mailman on the porch. That damn wheelchair really got him fucked up in the head."

She started to cry from expressing her man's hell.

"He's always talking about not being able to run around after the baby and being able to please me the way he used to."

"Hold up! He still works down there, don't he? I mean, I'm not trying to be all up in yo' shit, but I'm just trying to understand why he feels like that," I explained, before I scooped up a mouthful of my food.

"I know. And, yeah, I hop my big ass on that dick whenever and however he wants me to, so it's not that."

"Roc likes to be in control, so I can see why that shit got bro fucked up. I wish the nigga would let us come over there.

Hell! We family too!" Apple said, taking a seat at the table with me.

"Ya know what? We all just gonna pop up over there later with drinks and food and shit. I'ma get his ass high as a muthafucka and show his fool ass that he's still one of us and we need him still," I told her.

And I wasn't going to take no for an answer, but she didn't give me one.

"Yeah, do that! It might be what his ass needs. I know his ass has been in a mood because money is tight. That's been another one of his rants and a big stressor."

We heard Lyte's name being called in the background, so I made her promise us she would call when she was done with her appointment. I wondered if money was tight for them, and why he hadn't come to me. Well, hell! He hadn't been talking to me or anybody else. I hoped that boy didn't think we were gonna look at him like he was a beggar or some shit!

"Apple, don't get too full. I think I need another lesson on how to make ya feel the way you made me last night."

I flirted to let her know that I didn't feel awkward about what we had done.

TWENTY-THREE

KADEEM/GULLY

I knew we were getting close to needing to re-up, so I reached out to see what I could come up with right here just until we heard from J. Ross or found a connect just as good. Papa Luv put together a meeting with a young dope boy named Buck. It wasn't like I didn't know who he was. I think the whole damn city knew him and his Wildwayz clique. I wouldn't deal with him because of a few of the stories of how hot-headed he was. But right now he had the best work in the city besides ours, and the numbers weren't too bad.

"Man, get up out the pussy and meet me at Mom's daycare. I got something lined up for us right here that we need to check out. If it's as good as what Papa showed me just now, we won't have to hit the highway."

"I'm with that, but gimme about an hour. I just walked into the barber shop, and there's a chair open," Gully explained as he sat in the chair of one of our best barbers.

"Fo' sho! Handle yo' shit and meet me there. I'ma put up yo' part so we can leave when you get there."

I tossed in the whole amount needed for the purchase in a

black knapsack and headed out to my truck. Gully agreed and then ended the call so he could get cut up.

"Tee, why is it so hot in this bitch?" he asked the barber as he placed the cloth over his shoulders.

"It's hot because yo' ass never got the air conditioner fixed when I told you about it acting up."

"Man, ya know I be high right? Anyway, that's what yo' ass is here for. To cut hair and to make sure everything runs smoothly around here. I won't trip as long as ya keep the paperwork when ya have something done."

"I know; that's why I ordered two new ones. They should be here sometime today to put 'em in," Tee informed him, with an unlit blunt hanging out from the corner of his mouth.

Gully met Tee a few years back at the probation office. Tee was fresh out of Green Bay Correctional Institution where he learned how to cut hair and do everything else about cosmetology. We were in the market for something to invest in that would not only clean up our money but also be profitable. So Gully thought about opening up a barbershop. I found a spot on Fond du Lac, and we never looked back. The shop stayed packed because all they did in there was bet on games, blow loud, cut hair, and talk shit—in that order. For the most part, the shop was well respected by most. A few times guys had almost come to blows over petty stuff, but it never turned into gun play.

"How do you want this?" Tee asked, when he was done with Gully's head.

"Man, ya know shit don't change with me! Quit playin'."

"Hey, I wouldn't be a good barber if I didn't ask every now and then."

He then stepped back to study Gully's face before he went to work on his beard.

~ ~ ~

It was over half an hour later when Gully pulled up to the daycare center. I got my things and came right out knowing the thundering bass I was hearing was coming from him. Once I was outside, I saw that Gully was driving his candy-painted gunmetal-and-soft-blue Camaro.

"We gotta meet up with Buck at Papa's spot on Center," I told him when I got in the car. "He says he got whatever for the low."

"What Buck ya talking 'bout? Wildwayz Buck or EGS Buck?" he inquired while pulling away from the daycare center.

"Wildwayz! Gully, we don't gotta let him know how we get down with this shit fo' real, fo' real, just that we serious until we can hit that E way. Shit, I still ain't heard from Ross, and if we keep waiting, we gonna be hit."

"Ya right, my nigga. But I'm keeping my burner on me just in case the nigga wanna try some of that wild shit."

Gully agreed with me and then unmuted the music to let me know that it wasn't up for discussion.

The meeting went well. We walked in planning on copping three bricks, and we walked out with four and a new respect for Buck. He turned out to be a real businessman once we sat down at the table. The look and scent of the product told me it was good. Papa Luv snorted a line from one of the bricks right in front of us and then gave us his approval. By the end of the meeting, Gully pretty much tossed out all the issues he had with doing business with Buckwild.

"So how ya feel about fucking with 'em?" I asked Gully once we were in the privacy of the Camaro, to be sure of my observation.

"Shit, I'm good as long as he keeps it the way he did just now. When ya went to get the cash, I had a talk with him."

"About what?"

"Kadeem, just know that the nigga respect my thug, feel me?"

I shook my head, but whatever they talked about wasn't stopping shit, and I was good with that. I was out there to get that cash. That's it. That's all!

TWENTY-FOUR

GP

Creamy excitedly entered the house and quickly closed and locked the door behind her, and then rushed into the living room.

"GP, it's good you're here. Where's everybody else?"

She dropped her overnight bag next to the couch where I was sitting and breaking down a blunt.

"We all here. What the fuck's wrong with you?" I asked, noticing she was unable to sit still.

"Ohhh, GP! I was just with that bitch-ass nigga's sister!"

"Bitch, calm down! Who ya talking about?"

"That punk that killed daddy. I was just with his dyke sister, Annasta, and her bitch."

I jumped to my feet as soon as the words left her lips.

"What bitch? Where?"

"Hold up and let me tell everybody together."

We went into Wonda's room where she was pulling out outfits for the day and telling Apple about her night with Gully. Once Creamy had our attention, she gave us the details of her night with Marci and Annasta.

"Bitch! Why the fuck didn't you call us so we could murder them hoes and they bitch-ass brother?" Wonda angrily demanded.

"Ma, I didn't call because them hoes are dumb as hell. They took me to a house that had plenty of dope and stacks of money just sitting out on a pool table."

"And, bitch, what's that mean?" Apple asked with rage in her eyes.

"And, I did what daddy taught me to do. I planned our next lick. Calboy would want us to get that and our get-back. I didn't wanna be like Candi's punk ass and not get the whole layout of the spot either way."

"Creamy, I like the way you think. We do need to get back on our shit. Lyte and Roc need us, since neither one of them can do shit for themselves right now, so ya did good!"

"Yeah! You did right, Creamy. I should've heard ya out before I got on you," Apple apologized.

"This shit could work real well. B. Burns and his sister do shit together for what I know about their hustle. So if we time it just right, we can kill that muthafucka and get paid all at once!" I spoke up taking charge.

"So, GP, how do ya wanna do this shit?" Wonda asked.

"First off, we need to hear more about this spot and see if

we can find out where the nigga moved to, just in case we can't catch him there."

"I got that covered. I already set up another date with them for when I got back from my booking in Fort Wayne."

"Yeah, cancel that shit. We need to get right on this shit here," Apple told her.

"Nope, don't cancel! Keep the booking. Ain't gonna rush this shit; and remember, we need all the money we can get."

"GP, if ya worried about Lyte, I got 'em. They can have what I got stashed here to hold them over. I know me and the girls can make all that shit right back, plus she said there was a lot of cash in the spot. We'll be good."

"I hear you, Wonda, but that's not what I'm talking about. I need to know that we all ready to do this shit, because there ain't no room for fuck-ups."

I looked at Apple and asked, "Can you show me ya ready to get back down?"

"Yes! Yeah, I'm ready. I'll do what I need to do to get shit done. I know my place," she answered and then dropped her head.

Her demeanor somehow made me think she was talking about what happened between us last night and, hell, again this morning.

"No, no, boo! Pick yo' head up. This ain't no pimp-hoe shit anymore. This is us doing what we gotta do as the unit— the family that Cal made us into. Just because he's not here don't mean everything has to fall apart. We all still need to play our parts. I got this when it comes to doing these licks. You and Creamy keep bringing them in, and Wonda keeps doing what she always has."

"No, fuck that, GP! I'm ready to bring Juicy outta retirement and go out with y'all. Remember, I started this shit with Cal. I ain't no punk bitch. I'm good as long as I hit mom's hand for taking care of the kids, and she's straight. Plus y'all need me, since Roc and Lyte are out."

"Okay, well you and her need to show me y'all ready then. I got something I've been peeping for some time now. I ain't ever said nothing about it because bro wouldn't want to do it because we can't get eyes on the inside, but I know we can pull it off easy."

I gave them the details of what I had in mind. When I was done, Juicy went and took a chair out into the hallway so she could open the panel in the ceiling that led to the attic. She then reached in and removed a small duffel bag and dropped it onto the floor.

"This is my just-in-case stash, or to-go pack as Cal liked

to call it."

She smiled and unzipped it, and pulled out thick bundles of cash. Juicy replaced two of the seven bundles and gave the rest to Roc and Lyte for them and the baby.

"I know I said they could have it all, but a bitch gotta have something at all times."

"It's all good. I'ma hit them with something too. I got a to-go pack myself," I told her.

We then all started getting ready for our visit with Roc, just like I had promised Lyte earlier in the day.

TWENTY-FIVE

KADEEM/GULLY

Gully hated to leave his gun in the car, but he respected the no-firearm rule in the studio because he was a personal friend of the owner and the studio did have armed security.

"What it do! I smell it. Let a thug hit that there y'all smoking on?" he greeted the crew when he walked into the smoke-filled room.

"Gully, ya right on time. I'm 'bout to end this nigga in the booth's time right now. So you can get ready to hop right in there."

"Cool, cool! Is this lil nigga hot? Let me hear that shit," he said to one of the engineers sitting down next to a few other guys in the room and rolling his own blunt of the weed they had tossed to him.

I got da city on lock, 24 tic-tock
Seven days a week, nigga cooking up that wop
These cold streets stay hot, so I keep that flip flop
That's that DE, bang, make a nigga heart stop

Highland Park street kings, some say dream team

I'm ridin' on them big wheels, iced out, bling bling

Back to back, hood to hood, penetrate the projects

Investin' on my profits bring it to yo' doorstep

Al Capone, Gotti, Lucky Lu, me I'm on some mob shit

Yo baby mama and her friend, love to ride Gully dick

Two cell phones, pistol on me, and a pair of dice

Smokin' on that good dro, we call that shit paradise

Couple rubber bandz, for the chain and wrist watch

I started from the bottom, I'ma finish on the damn top

Get money, get money, get money

It's ya boy, Gully, I'm the truth in these streets

If a nigga wanna beef, I get loose with these heats

By any means necessary, yeah we gone eat

Niggas hustle all night, niggas never gone sleep

Get money, get money, get money . . . .

"Whoa! Whoa! Whoa! Hold up right there, Gully," the engineer interrupted him in the middle of his flow.

"This shit hot, right, but I think ya should make that last part the hook."

Gully turned his black Gucci cap backward. "Okay! Play the part ya talking 'bout back for me." He stepped back from the mic head waiting for the play back.

"Alright, 'Paid in Full,' hook round one," the engineer announced, and then played back his suggestion for the hook.

Get money, get money, get money

It's ya boy, Gully, I'm the truth in these streets

If a nigga wanna beef, I get loose with these heats

By any means necessary, yeah we gone eat

Niggas hustle all night, niggas never gone sleep.

"Talk to me, my nig! What ya think?" he asked Gully.

"Let's do it. I came to work today, my nigga. Hey, hey! Why don't one of y'all order us some pizzas and shit on me. And I'ma need some more of that lemony loud pack too. I'm in this bitch all night," Gully answered excitedly.

~ ~ ~

It had been a week since Vudu connected with Candi at the club, and she had her mind on winning him over. Candi liked his swagger and felt safe around Vudu and his goons. Her plan was to prove to him why he should keep her around. She had already given him most of the money she made from her last two nights of stripping and turning her dates on the side. Now she was showing him how she could get money another way.

"Bitch, hurry the fuck up! I got shit to do!" Vudu snapped.

"Okay, daddy! I only got two more ATMs to hit, and I'm done with these cards."

"Whatever, Candi! Just hurry the fuck up."

"Don't be like that! I'm doing this for you, daddy!" Candi spoke to Vudu through her Bluetooth earpiece as she walked away from the ATM booth, scanning the crowd of pedestrians for any sign of trouble as she went.

Nobody seemed to be interested in what she had done. Then suddenly a police car bent the corner with its lights flashing causing her heart to race. Candi hurried to the car, and Vudu pulled off into the heavy downtown traffic. The police didn't stop at the bank or follow. They shot past them in a hurry to get someplace else.

"Bitch, why's your heart beating so fast? You thought they was coming for your bad ass, didn't you?" Vudu teased Candi, and then began laughing at her as he drove.

"Ohhhh, that ain't funny! I didn't know!" she replied, and then laughed with him. "Can we stop and get something to eat?" she asked while pointing at a Burger King coming up ahead.

"Yeah, you read my mind. I was starting to think yo' pretty

ass only ran off dick!" he joked as his phone rang.

"Wow! I can't believe you said that," she laughed as he took the call. "But for real, it is a big part of my diet."

Vudu shook his head. "What up, fam? Tell a nigga something good!" he said to his caller.

"I got something good for you. I just got off with folks down the way. He said ole boy just got down there. Me and fam are on our way down the way now. What ya want us to do if the nigga's leaving when we get there?" Jazz asked.

"What ya think, nigga? Don't let him get away from y'all. Put his shit on flat if ya gotta, but just don't let him get away before I get there."

"Alright! We on it! "Jazz assured him and then ended the call.

Vudu was so excited to get the news about Gully, that he pulled off from Burger King without his food or Candi.

"Oh shit!" he said when she called his phone. "My bad, ma! Here I come now."

He ended the call before she could say something smart-mouthed to him and made a U-turn to go back for her. On his way back, he wondered what he was going to do with Candi once he was done with his contact. Would he leave her or keep her online?

~ ~ ~

At the studio, Gully was still going strong in the sound booth.

"Say, my nigga. Since you on a roll right now, why don't ya spit that one joint, 'Reckless,' you don't like, so my nigga can hear it?"

"Ya know all you gotta do is put on the beat and I'm gone," he answered in between a much-needed drink of his Arizona Sweet Tea.

"Okay, when you ready. 'Reckless,' round one," the engineer said and then let the beat play.

"Alright, I'm reckless! Hey, turn it up a little bit," Gully requested before going into the hook.

I'm screamin' yolo, yolo, yolo, reckless
Ya only live once, is what my nigga told me
There's a life after death is what the preacher showed me
So I stash away cash for the weekend
So I can blow some bud and pop bottles with current
friends
All I ever thought about was dollar signs and sleepin' in
And now I'm lookin' at my past life from a Wisconsin pen
Damn!

I should've known that even life got a reflext
I was fooled, the nigga played it cool and hit me with a
pretext
Was caught up in a wave of deceit but never the loss
Continued runnin' wicked in the streets
Boss so guess what happen next.
Reckless . . . .

~ ~ ~

Gully exited the studio and found his Camaro on two flats. "What the fuck!" he cussed while pulling a small steak knife from his 26-inch tire.

After Gully looked around and pulled out his cell to call for a ride and a tow, he noticed a man dressed in dark colors enter the alley and then another coming his way from between some apartment buildings. Gully knew right away that they had something to do with his flat tires. But the only thing he was mad about was that somebody had caught up with him without his gun instead of it being the other way around. Knowing he could get in the car and get it before they got up on him, he tried to pretend like the car wasn't his and quickly turned and walked away from it heading toward the opposite end of the alley where another man entered.

"Hold up! Don't move, bitch-ass nigga! J. Ross sent us!" Vudu stated, removing his gun from the pocket of his black hoody as he headed in Gully's direction.

"Fuck ya talking 'bout? Ross knows how to get up with me. What's this shit about?" he demanded, knowing it couldn't be good.

"Lay the fuck down and we'll talk 'bout that."

"Fuck you! That shit there ain't gonna happen," Gully responded after seeing the goons had him boxed in.

He knew there was no way in hell he could take them without his gun.

As they got closer to him, Gully hated that he didn't keep the knife, because it would have come in handy in the confrontation that was about to happen. He knew they wanted to try to take him alive or he would have been dead already. Just as he readied himself to put up his fight, a police officer crept up on all of them and ordered them to drop their guns and get down on the ground.

This was a kind of miracle to Gully, or the luckiest night of his life. When Vudu turned and ran, Gully took that as his cue and ran as well. Only he went in the opposite direction as the rest of them. By the time he made it to Wisconsin Avenue, he heard a few gunshots and prayed they weren't aiming for him.

"Lord, please don't let them shoot me in the back," he prayed to himself as he sprinted safely away.

TWENTY-SIX

KADEEM

I was home chillin' taking a break from all the running I had done today. The work I bought from Buckwild didn't slow business down one bit.

"How long you gonna be here? I bought something, and I want ya to tell me what you think about it," Lady said while walking into the kitchen and finding me getting a cold beer.

"I don't know, but I know I always got a minute for you," I answered, trying to get a few points in for when we went to bed later.

With all the work I put in today, I planned on getting something tonight.

"You better." She smiled. "Come on!"

I followed her into our bedroom, where she quickly picked up a bag off the bed.

"What ya hiding?"

"Boy, I'm not hiding shit. I just don't want you to see it until I'm ready. Now sit down and wait!" she ordered before dashing into the bathroom.

"Hey, did they ever come to fix the washing machine, or

do I gotta go up there and get me some ass?"

I picked up her tablet off the bed to do a little snooping. Lady was always buying online, and I was just checking to see what she was on.

"Yeah, it was fixed yesterday. I thought I told you that," she answered through the bathroom door.

"Lady, why you looking at foreclosed houses? What's on yo' mind?"

"Stop looking at my shit with yo' nosey ass. I'ma talk to you about that when you get in the house for the night."

Well, I knew if I didn't go with whatever she was on with this, I wouldn't be getting none from her tonight. Maybe I should try to get me a quickie now since I'm here.

The door opened up and Lady walked out wearing a lacy, emerald-and-tan bra and panty set with a pair of four-inch gold Jimmy Choo heels.

"What do you think about this?"

"What you mean? Damn, bae! Ya looking like one of them Vicki models."

I was already a horny muthafucka when I walked into the house. Now seeing her in this had me hard as a brick.

"Okay, but do that mean ya like it or not?"

She did a slow turn for me.

"Come here and let me see."

I almost growled in lust as she motioned me over.

As Lady walked slowly over to my side of the bed, she put a little extra sway in her hips for my pleasure. I pulled her between my legs, filled my hands with her soft butt, and kissed her lustfully.

Without breaking the kiss, I dragged my hands hungrily up her back and around to her waiting nipples. She put her hands up my shirt, pulling it over my head and dropping it onto the bed.

"Tell me you want me, Kadee!" she demanded, bracing her hands on my shoulders as her knees got weak from my lips on her chest and my hands working her nipples.

"Ain't I showing you that now?" I unhooked her bra and took a nipple in my mouth. "Here, let me show ya better." I stood up and dropped my jeans and my boxers, freeing my hardness.

Lady licked her lips at the sight of it. She then grabbed it and kissed me some more. I dipped my fingers into her panties, just loving how wet she was. That's when I heard Gully's ringtone playing on my phone. But I wasn't gonna stop to answer for him. Instead I pulled her moist panties aside and then scooped her up by her butt. I then lowered her down until I felt my tip parting her wetness. Lady wrapped her legs around my waist, and I went deep until I felt her nails digging into my shoulders.

~ ~ ~

When Gully told me about what had happened to him, I felt bad for not picking up the phone that night. He really felt like they wanted to kill him. I didn't debate with him on it; instead, I just agreed and told my nigga that we needed to get ready for war if that's what J. Ross wanted with us. But why? That was the question we had to try to find out.

Just because we were both seasoned hustlers didn't mean we were too proud to ask for help. Hell! Proud niggas get killed in times like this, but real men persist. I made Lady take time off work and sent her and my kids to stay with my godmother until me and Gully could get things worked out with the bloodthirsty kingpin.

Gully had KC put all of our goons on full alert so they would be ready to put in the work when that time came. We put up our nice vehicles and bought two dependable cheap used cars so we could move around more incognito. I bought a Buick LeSabre that came with a pretty good radio, because I think better with my music. Gully got himself a trusty Chevy

Malibu and then had both of our cars' windows darkly tinted. I still had some explaining to do with Lady and Moms, so I headed that way while Gully went to pay his uncle a visit to let him know what was going on with us and see if he could give him advice on how to go about handling it.

"Boy, how did y'all get in that bullshit with Ross?" Uncle Earl asked in shock at what Gully told him about the run-in with the hit squad that claimed to be sent by J. Ross. "This nigga's a fool."

"Unc! I know. I don't know why he's coming for us like this and shit. On my life, Unc! I don't know."

"Did some shit go down that ya wasn't supposed to see?" he asked while using the pool stick he was holding to lean on.

"Nope! The last time we saw him, he was surrounded by the Feds and shit!" When telling his uncle that story, it made him think. "Do ya think the nigga thinks we had something to do with that shit?"

"I was just about to ask you that myself."

When Gully didn't respond, his uncle asked, "Well, did y'all have something to do with it?"

"Really, Unc? Ya really gonna ask me something like that? I'm real in this game and in life. That shit there's cray."

His uncle didn't reply. He just kept looking him in the eyes and waiting for the answer.

"Hell no, Unc! I ain't have shit to do with it, and neither did Kadeem! I put my life on that."

"Okay, I believe you. I just had to hear the words from you before I jump and put myself out there on this shit."

"Well now ya know! So tell me what I'm supposed to do?"

He could see that Gully was angry and eager to get to the bottom of what was going on.

"Lil G, I still got a little pull in the city. Let me get with my folks and see if they can set it up so I can holla at Ross. If I can find out if he thinks y'all put them people on him, I'm sho I can get this shit cleared up. But, G, ya better be sure yo' boy ain't have shit to do with no rat shit. You muthafuckas ain't together 24/7."

"I know him like I know myself, and there ain't no rat in me," he said as his expression relaxed. "Good looking on this! Call me as soon as ya know something. I'ma be in the city for a day or two, just so you know where I'm at."

"What you going down there for when you just told me the nigga Ross is trying to kill you?" his uncle asked, setting down his empty beer mug.

"My future baby mama's down there. I'm good, Unc. He's looking for us up here, not down them ways; and she ain't no ghetto chick, so I'm good."

His uncle never heard him talk about a woman without calling her a bitch or hoe, so he knew the girl had to be special to him.

"Hold on, nephew. Before ya go running off, I gotta teach ya a lesson, and I think about five G's would be a good lesson for ya," he told him with a smile showing off his four gold teeth—two at the top and two at the bottom of his mouth.

"Unc! Instead of beating 'round the bush when ya low on cash, just ask me. I'll never turn ya down on some real shit. If I got it, you got it," Gully said, removing a nice wad of cash from his pocket.

"I know, nephew, but we family and got the same pride in us. I'm yo' uncle, and I shouldn't have to come to you every time I'm low. It should be the other way round. Nephew, back when yo' dad was living, we used to get it! We had bitches falling all over us. But when my brother died, I just lost it."

"Ya don't gotta explain, Unc."

He handed him $500.

"This is for now. I'ma have one of my niggas bring ya the rest ASAP."

They shook hands and hugged before Gully exited the bar. Gully made a promise to himself that he would start to come see his uncle more often.

Earl excused himself from the rest of the pool game he was playing when Gully walked in. He had to pay out the $50 they were betting, but he knew he would win it right back after he made the calls he needed to make to get in touch with J. Ross.

Once the call was made, Earl texted Gully and told him that he reached out to his old friend, and he told him that he would have J. Ross give him a call. Earl told Gully he would hit him as soon as that happened and to have me get up with him before he went outta town. Gully agreed, and then the wait was on.

TWENTY-SEVEN

GP

The following day after we made the surprise visit to see Roc and give him the money to hold them over, I had an idea on how to make Roc know that he was still part of the team. I went over and loaded him and his wheelchair into my car and took him to the site of the spot I had picked out for me and the girls to hit.

"How do you think we should go about getting in that bitch?" I asked him, reaching for the blunt he was smoking.

"We gotta sit on this bitch for a while and see how much in-and-out traffic there is, since we can't get nobody inside."

I had all that info already, but I didn't tell him that, because just as I thought, it was what he needed to pick up his spirits. Well, that and to smoke on some good kush. Roc's mood changed as soon as he smelled it in the air when we intruded in on his pity-party. I couldn't believe it when he told me how some of the same muthafuckas that bought weed from him ran off on him. I took him to ride down on them fools to get his money. It almost felt like the old days when me and Roc would ride and smoke, and then dump off whatever product we got off the licks that Calboy put us on. I said *almost*. This was a new day, and I was going to show them all that we were gonna be alright as long as we stayed together.

~ ~ ~

Vudu had Candi get him a rental car for a few days because he wasn't sure if the police got a good look at his Jeep the night Gully slipped through his fingers. When Candi pulled up to the apartment she was now sharing with Vudu in a dark blue GMC Envoy, Vudu and his cousins were standing outside smoking and talking shit as usual.

She honked the horn to get their attention while simultaneously rolling down the dark window.

"Is this good, daddy?" she yelled out when she had their full attention.

All three thugs marched over to the SUV and got in.

"Your ass must got some good credit with them son of a bitches down there. They told me all that was left were economy cars," Bay complained from the backseat.

"Nigga, look at my bitch and tell me she ain't got what she needs to get whatever she wants from them freaky-ass white folks in that bitch!" Vudu told him, before telling Candi that

ALL WORK, NO PLAY

he approved of it.

"Hey, since we in this bitch, let's ride down the way and grab another couple of zips of this good kush right quick," Jazz urged them, already texting on his phone to see if it was okay to come through.

"That's about the best shit ya had to say all day, fam. Straight up!" Bay teased.

"Fuck you!" Jazz responded and then told Candi the address of where to go.

Not long after they were stopping outside of the spot, Candi's punk ass whispered into Vudu's ear that she had $1,000 on her and she wanted to get some weed to sell to the girls at the club when she went to work that night.

"Folks ask 'em if I can get a couple of zips of that shit too."

"Hell, just come in with me. He knows y'all good if ya with me. Nigga ain't gonna turn down no cash on hand ever," Jazz said before exiting the truck.

Out of pure habit, Vudu pulled on his gloves and checked his gun before getting out.

"You stay out here just in case these niggas ain't as cool as cuzo thinks they is about meeting new faces," he told Candi.

She saw a gun lying on the seat when he got up.

"Daddy?"

When he looked back in the SUV, Candi pointed to it.

"I'm good, ma. I only need this one."

"Well, I'ma hold this one down just in case I gotta come in that bitch to get y'all. A bitch be in there like boom-boom on them hoes!" she said while playing with the gun.

"Be cool with that. It's loaded, and there ain't no safety on it!" he warned her before he caught up with his guys on the porch of the spot.

Not one of them noticed us parked in the car on the opposite corner from them. When I saw how carelessly the guy in the spot opened the door, I decided it was time to make our move. I told Lyte to find us a good place to park in the back of the house so we could have an easier getaway when we came running out from that bitch. Her pregnant ass insisted we let her drive since we decided that Creamy should stay focused on getting all the information she could on B. Burns. So it was just Juicy, Apple, and me going in.

"It's go time! Once we get outta this car, ain't no backing out. So if y'all ain't ready, speak up."

"GP, shut that shit up and let's go get this money!" Juicy spoke up as she pulled down her mask to be sure it was on good when it was time to use it.

"Apple, change of plans. You stay out here and make sure don't no muthafuckas sneak in the back on us."

"Alright! I'ma be ducked on the side of the house."

She casually broke away from us to take her position.

"Bitch, ya ready to do this?"

"Wonda, quit playing with me. Bitch, ya know I'm trained to go!" I said.

I then pulled down my mask and hit the door that I saw them carelessly open so many times before tonight.

~ ~ ~

Jazz and the doorman jerked their heads toward the door when they heard rushing footsteps on the porch. Before they knew what was going down, the flimsy door burst open. Vudu pulled his gun and sent shots at the door while ducking out of my line of fire. We returned fire, dropping the two closest to us.

This was not what I expected it to be. I knew I should grab my girl and get the fuck outta there, but I was the one who picked this and I needed to show the others I wasn't all talk. Juicy was true to what she had said about being ready. She busted her gun and pushed farther into the house.

Annasta picked up one of the guns from the pool table and ran for the back door with her brother.

"Come on! Let's get outta here!"

"What about Marci?" B. Burns asked, not slowing his escape.

Vudu followed right behind them.

"What the fuck is this shit?" he asked. "They killed my cousin!" he said, sending a few shots in back of him to slow down any other followers.

"I think it's just a robbery. I thought this shit was y'all at first!" Annasta admitted to him once the three of them were in the back hallway.

She lowered her gun to show that she wasn't on no bullshit with him.

"Let's just get the fuck outta here!"

B. Burns was sweating so badly at this point that it looked like someone had hit him with a water balloon.

Back in the house, I helped Juicy gather up the cash and drugs that we came for. Out of the corner of my eyes, I caught two females stepping out of the bedroom, and I quickly sent two shots their way.

"Whoa, whoa! Y'all stop! It's me!" Creamy said, pushing

away from the girl who she was with.

"What the fuck? You bitch! You set us up!" Marci screamed as she ran toward Creamy.

"Bitch, stop!"

I shot her in the face just because I knew she had to be the bitch Marci that Creamy had told us she was with.

"Creamy, is that bitch-ass nigga in there?"

"No! He was out here somewhere."

"Fuck! I let that bitch get away!"

I was pissed. Thinking we were the only ones left standing, Creamy started helping us gather up what we came for. She went back in the room where she and Marci were hiding to get two bags—one brown paper and the other a black trash bag.

"Wonda, look out!" Creamy screamed when she saw one of the goons who was playing dead try to aim his gun.

"Noooo!" I screamed, firing shots into his body until I saw nothing but blood. "Let's go now!"

We ran back out the way we came in.

~ ~ ~

B. Burns opened the back door and was met face-to-face by a wasted Apple. She didn't hesitate when she saw the man who was the cause of all of her pain. Apple blew his brains all over the person behind him. When Annasta saw her brother go down, she froze for a second in shock. Vudu pushed past her and punched Apple hard enough to knock her off her feet. He then made a dash for the front door, where Candi was supposed to be waiting. But when she saw us kick in the door, she drove around the back thinking that her guys would run out that way.

"Bitch, I'ma kill you!" Annasta roared before jumping on Apple as she was trying to pick herself up off the ground.

"Bitch! Bitch! Bitch!" was all she kept saying as she rained blows on Apple's arms as she did her best to block her face.

"No!" Apple yelled, when the crazed sibling started to aim her gun.

That's when Candi appeared and shot Annasta in the back. She did not stop pulling the trigger until she heard the gun click empty.

Apple got to her feet and the two locked eyes before she turned and ran. Candi did the same, only she was going after her man. Once she was back in the SUV, she took off in the direction she saw Vudu run.

~ ~ ~

A squad car in the area responding to the call from the shot spotter cut off Vudu as he ran with his gun in hand searching for Candi. The hardened thug fired at the police car and ran the other way.

By this time, a few other of B. Burns and Annasta's goons showed up and started at him just because they didn't know him. Vudu shot back until his gun was empty. The men had him pinned down behind a parked car. He wasn't just going to sit there until they realized he wasn't responding with shots of his own anymore and come kill him. Instead, he sprang to his feet and made a run for it, at the same time Candi rounded the corner. Vudu then ran toward her.

"Where are you, Vu?" Candi asked herself, before she spotted him coming her way with a gunner about to fire on him.

She put the pedal to the floor and flew past her man, smacking two of the guys who were behind him. Vudu saw what she had done for him, but he didn't have time to admire her work. He jumped into the truck.

"Go! Go! Get the fuck outta here!" he ordered.

"What about Jazz?" she asked, hesitating a second too long for him.

Vudu smacked her upside her head.

"Bitch, I said go!" he reacted and got the action he was looking for.

Candi smashed on the gas again and didn't stop until all of the action was behind them.

TWENTY-EIGHT

KADEEM/GULLY

Gully stood in prayer with Alima admiring the beautiful harmonic recital of the opening prayer inside the motel they were sharing for his visit. She wouldn't allow him to spend as much on a room the way he had on his last two visits. Bro thought it was her way of showing him that she wasn't with him for his cash.

Bismillaahir rahmaanir raheem
alhamdu lillaahi rabbil aalameen
arrahmaanir raheem
maaliki yawmid deen
iyyaaka na'budu wa iyyaaka nasta'een
ihdinaas siraatal mustageem
siraatal ladheena an'amta 'alayhim ghairil maghdoobi
'alayhim wa laad daalleen
Ameen.

"Gully, let's go out somewhere. I know a good sports bar where we can eat and watch the game."

"Sounds good to me. I hope the food is good, cause a nigga about hostage hungry," Gully replied while watching Alima as she removed the long sleeper she was wearing.

"Let's hold off on that a bit. I just seen something else I got a taste for," he told her as he got up from his seat in the firm motel chair and walked up on her.

She turned just as his arms went around her waist.

"What happened to you being so hostage hungry?" she asked, giggling as he tickled her earlobe and neck with his tongue.

"Come here! Let me show you how hungry I am."

He didn't wait for her response. He just scooped her into his arms and then turned and tossed her onto the unmade bed. He then roughly dragged her to the edge and buried his head deep between her knees.

~ ~ ~

The devious detective made his way through the crowded bar and took a seat. He continued to scan the rowdy establishment for his confidential informant, when he felt a hand on his shoulder from behind him.

"What ya drinking?"

The detective turned to face the owner of the hand, already

knowing whose voice it was. "I'm drinking nothing but the best, if you're the one paying?"

"Don't I always?"

"You know what? I never noticed," the detective chuckled. "And now that you offered, I'll take whatever that is you're drinking. Tell me you got something to smoke?"

"It all depends on what ya trying to smoke. Since I'm quickly becoming your one-stop pleasure shop."

"If you got any issues with our relationship, I can always take you back to my place so we can talk there."

"It ain't no need for threats. Just tell me what the fuck you want. Damn!"

"Say, my man, give me a pack of them Marlboro Lights and a bag of chips," the detective told the bartender, who was busy making his drink. "I hope you got something for me— info or cash. I can use the cash more right about now."

"It's been kinda touchy on the streets lately, but I thought you might want me to hit yo' grimy-ass hand." The informant's cell started to vibrate on his thigh. He pulled it out of his pocket and recognized the number. "Hold that thought. I gotta take this."

"Whoa, whoa! Tell your girlfriend you'll be home with the milk after you give me my money."

"This ain't my bitch, and yo' money in the car. Just drink yo' drink and tell me who winning the game when I get back. Shit! Ya might just get both of what you want." He turned briskly away, pushing his way outside to return the call.

~ ~ ~

After an hour of burning off the last of whatever energy they had in the bed, the two lovebirds were finally out front of the sports bar looking for a place to park.

"Yeah! This what I'm talking 'bout. This muthafucka look like it's jumpin'."

"Yeah, it's always live when our boys are playin'," Alima bragged as she found a good slot right in front of the big picture window.

That's when Gully noticed someone he knew.

"Say! We can't stay here, but hold up. I wanna see something."

"Gully, what's wrong?" she asked, quickly scanning the crowded sidewalk and the cars in the area.

"Ya know that situation I told you that I didn't wanna talk about? Part of it is standing over there," he told her as he pointed toward Big Ed.

"Well, if that's him, you said it was some kinda misunderstanding, right? So, go talk to him and clear it up."

"I plan on it, but a nigga can't just go running up on a nigga in their backyard. I gotta sit back and observe," he explained as he reached between her legs and grabbed his gun from under her seat.

"Something told me not to leave home without my bitch," Gully griped while clicking off the safety.

"Gully, do you really think you gonna need that? Look! There are too many people out here for him to try anything, and there's a detective standing by the door."

"How do you know that's a detective?" Gully asked, just as he saw Big Ed and the white man walk toward a row of parked cars.

"I remember him from when my brother got caught with drugs at school a few months back. He was cool about it and just let me take him home instead of giving him a felony."

"That's good to know. Now stay here. I'ma try it yo' way and go try to talk with him."

Gully slid out of the car and made his way over to where Big Ed and Dickerson were standing next to a cream-colored Infiniti EX35. As he got closer, he noticed Big Ed hand the detective an envelope.

Dickerson took the envelope and inspected the contents. "This'll work." He removed the stack of cask and then crumpled the envelope. "I need you to understand that you don't run shit. I'm the boss here, homeboy." Dickerson threw away the trash, hitting Big Ed in the chest.

"I hope I'm not interrupting something big!" Gully asked, making his presence known as he walked up from between the parked cars.

"Ed, we need to talk ASAP."

"It's okay. We're done here. Ed, just give me a call when you can, so we can do this again soon." The shifty detective turned and then left the two alone.

Once the cop was out of hearing range, Gully asked Big Ed what was going on. "What's up, my nigga? Why y'all got muthafuckas looking for us and shit?"

"First off, don't be running up on me. And I don't got nobody looking for you. You muthafuckas need to holla at Jay 'bout that shit there." As soon as the words left his mouth, he thought of what just took place with the detective in front of Gully. "Why don't you let me know where ya gonna be at, and I'll have him get up with you in person."

"Do you take me for a fool, nigga? I ain't telling you where I'm staying, so ya can send somebody else at me. That nigga know our numbers. Tell him to call us. And don't worry, I won't say shit about yo' friend the detective," Gully informed him, letting him know that he knew Dickerson was the police.

"Nigga, ya need to mind yo' business and watch yo' words. Some may take that as a threat and send more of them niggas to holla at you."

Gully heard him, but he didn't respond. Bro just wanted to get back to the car so he could get his phone to call me and let me know what he just witnessed.

~ ~ ~

"So, how did it go?" Alima asked once Gully made it back to the car, where she was waiting and watching when he went over to talk to Big Ed.

"It's all good. And just like ya said, there's way too many people out here for it to go any other way," he told her, pulling her in his arms for a kiss to stop her from asking him anything more. "Now let's get something to eat. You go get us a spot in there. I gotta make a call right quick."

Alima agreed and then started walking toward the entrance of the sports bar. As Gully retrieved his cell phone from the seat of the car, out of the corner of his eye he saw an SUV speeding toward them from the back of the lot.

"Alima, look out!" he yelled while running for her.

The truck flew by them so close that they could feel the rush of air as Gully pulled her out of the way.

The truck screamed to a hard stop, and its passenger door opened with a man hopping out and pointing a gun. Gully quickly dropped back and pulled his gun, exchanging fire with the goon. The battle stopped as quickly as it had started, and the cream-colored Infiniti raced off. Gully ran behind it a few steps, firing until his gun was empty. He wanted Big Ed to know that he wouldn't be easy to kill.

When he turned around, he saw Alima lying dead in the street. He knew that he couldn't be around when the police arrived. It broke his heart more to have to leave her lying alone in the street as he got into the car and raced away.

TWENTY-NINE

GP

I was shot in the thigh by a stray bullet as I ran away from the house. I felt extra tired and maybe weak from blood loss. I didn't know! But what I did know was that I couldn't go to the hospital or have us stopped by the police with these guns and drugs in the car. I then passed out.

"Lay her on the table and take her pants off," Roc ordered as he got ready to see if my wound needed a doctor or just someone to patch it up.

"Lyte, grab some cotton balls and alcohol and some hot water and stuff," Juicy ordered while helping Apple undress me.

Once my pants were off, Roc used them to clear away some of the blood so he could get a better look.

"It ain't too bad. She just got grazed, but it still looks pretty deep. She's definitely gonna need stitches."

"Okay! So, do you think we can take her to the hospital, or do we still gotta do it ourselves?" Juicy asked him.

"She can go to the hospital so she won't get infected. Just find her something else to put on, and give me the alcohol so

I can clean it and wrap it up."

I woke up screaming and swinging. I then hit Roc's hard-ass wheel on his chair and hurt my hand.

"Hold her arms down!" Roc told them, laughing as he poured some more of the alcohol on my leg.

"What's so funny, punk? You doing this shit on purpose?"

"Chill, GP! I ain't doing shit to try to hurt yo' ass. I'm just making sure it's clean enough before I wrap it up," he explained.

"How bad is it?" I asked, afraid to look down at it.

"It's just a deep gash from the bullet grazing you. We gonna take you to the hospital when he's done, so they can give you meds for the pain and so you won't get an infection," Juicy explained, keeping a tight grip on my arm so I wouldn't hit anyone.

I dressed myself, and then Apple drove me to the hospital.

"I didn't tell the others this yet because I was worried about you."

"You didn't tell the others what?" I asked, looking for the half blunt I knew I had in the ashtray of my car.

"I got 'em both. I killed that muthafucka that killed Cal, and Candi killed that bitch."

"Candi? What Candi are you talking about? I know you

ain't talking 'bout that dumb bitch that caused my brother his life?"

"GP, she saved me. Oh, girl was gonna shoot me, and outta nowhere Candi showed up and shot her."

For the first time I really took a look at Apple's face, and I could see that she had been in a fight.

"Where she go? Did she say anything to you?"

Apple turned into the busy hospital parking lot.

"I don't know. But she didn't say shit to me. She just ran off, and I went the other way."

I wonder why she was there. Was Candi trying to revenge bro's death and somehow knew where the nigga was?

"We gonna talk about this after I get outta here. Have them check you out too. Yo' face looks pretty bad."

"Okay." She then pulled me toward her and kissed me softly. "I'm glad you okay."

I kissed her again before we got out of the car, and she wheeled me inside in a wheelchair that she found parked outside the entrance. I guess this was now a full-blown relationship between us, which was something else we all needed to talk about soon.

THIRTY

KADEEM/J. ROSS

J Ross took into consideration Earl's plea for him to call off the contract on me and Gully. He then pieced together who the real rat was, after putting together the information that he had Sonya collect for him. But before he told Vudu to stand down, he needed to be sure.

"Sonya, do you know the reason why the fat boy ain't answering his phone?"

"No, but I'll try to call him from my line. His ass has been houndin' me for some of this good-good all week, so he may answer for me."

Sonya retrieved her cell from her Jimmy Choo bag and hit speed dial for Big Ed.

"Hey, I hate to fuck up yo' night, 'cause it sounds like y'all partying good, but Ross just called looking for you. He's wondering why you're not answering his calls," she said, telling a half-truth.

"Oh shit, Sonya! I don't got my other cell on me. I left it on the charger in the truck. I'ma call him ASAP. I need to holla at my boy about some shit that went down last night."

"What shit? What you talking 'bout?"

"It ain't nothing ya need to worry about. Do ya know what he wanna holla at me 'bout?" Big Ed asked, wondering if he heard about what went down outside of the bar.

"He didn't say. He just told me to have you call him. So call him now, Ed. I don't need him on my ass about you."

"I got you, Sonya. But the shit ya need to be thinking 'bout is putting that ass on this dick," he told her as he pulled his other cell phone out of his pocket.

"I'm for real. If I get in some shit with him, Ed, the only thing you gonna have in yo' lap is some ice," she promised before she ended the call.

"His fat ass should be calling you in a few. His lying ass said his phone is in his truck. You and I both know that nigga ain't going nowhere without them lines on him. He said some shit went down last night that he wanna talk to you about, but didn't say what it was."

While Sonya was on the phone with Ed, Ross was on the phone with the big man himself.

"Yeah, I wonder if it has anything to do with Salazar's call just now. I can't remember the last time he told me to come see him just outta the blue, and he ain't never told me to bring Ed along!"

"Whoa! It must be some real shit then. He really wants us to come down there, huh?"

"Us? You mean me and Ed, yes. But—!"

"But nothing, Jay! I'm coming with. Ya just said you don't know what it's about. So if it's some bullshit, I need to be there to do my job and bring you home."

"Sonya! Sonya!" he called her name forcefully to get her full attention. "Okay, ya right! But you going with Ed 'cause we can't have him suspicious of you before we know what he's been up to."

"I understand," she answered.

When Ross's cell phone began playing Big Ed's ringtone, Sonya reached over and undid his belt and pants. As soon as he began talking, Sonya buried her head into J. Ross's lap, taking his hardness between her full lips. She gave him head as he explained to Ed that the connect wanted to see them both.

"Our numbers are on point, so I don't know why he wants to see us both," Big Ed said.

"Well, who knows? This trip might be a reward or some shit. We'll talk then," J. Ross said, quickly ending the call and releasing into Sonya's wanting mouth.

~ ~ ~

After Gully told me what happened to his girl down the way, I had to go spend time with Lady because you never know what can happen. I feel for bro, but in a way it's good he hadn't known her long or he would be really fucked up in the head.

My phone rang the ringtone I had set for Buck.

"What it do, my nigga?"

"I need to holla at you right quick. Where can I ride down on you?"

"This must be some real shit if ya tryin' to see me in traffic."

"Yeah! it's 'bout yo' issue with them in the Windy. Don't ask how I know. Just tell me where I need to be so we can holla."

I told him to meet me at Culvers in Midtown.

"Bae, when my nigga gets here, I'ma need to go out and holla at him. He might have some info that can help end this chaos so we can get back to our life," I explained to Lady.

"Okay! I hope so, because I'm ready to go home and sleep in my own bed with my soon-to-be husband."

"Lady, it ain't that bad over at mama's, is it?" I asked just as our food was brought to the table.

"I'm not saying that. I'm just ready to go home and back

to work. I could've found a much better use for my time off, like on the beach somewhere nice with you or my other nigga," she joked.

"You must don't think I'll beat that ass about you giving away what's mine?"

"The last I checked, it was between my legs, not yours."

"I guess I need to get between them and see for myself. I can tell if somebody been in my shit."

Buck pulled into the parking lot two cars over from my car and called like I didn't see him. I told him I was on my way out, and then excused myself from Lady and went out to hear what he had to say.

"My nigga, I hear yo' people fuck with my people."

"What people you talking about? I fuck with a lot of mutha-fuckas in the Mil."

"I'm talking about our plugs. I just got a call earlier asking me what I know about you and Gully."

"Ya got a call from who, and what you mean?"

"Look, bruh, I'm on yo' side. My plug got word that you had issues with J. Ross. That's yo' plug, right?"

I didn't answer, and he took that as a yes.

"Anyway, I'm supposed to bring you in to have a sit-down so y'all can put an end to this misunderstanding. My plug knows who the rat is that got ya mixed up in all this. It's best for you to go down there and holla at him about this shit. And before ya ask, J. Ross will be there too."

"Alright, Buck. But ya know Gully's coming with us, and I should warn you now that he may try to get at Ross for killing his chick the other day."

"Hey, I'm just doing my part. The rest is on y'all. Just as long as we stay good."

I told him we were cool and then got out of his truck and called Gully before going back inside with Lady. The meeting was set up for tomorrow, so I took Lady home and made love to her like it was my last time. These were some powerful people we were about to sit down with, and if Gully took off and got to bustin' his guns, I was gonna follow suit.

THIRTY-ONE

KADEEM

J Ross, Big Ed, and Sonya were led by two armed men through the dimly lit warehouse to a solid wood door where one of the men knocked before opening it. He then waved them inside once he got the okay.

"Have a seat. Mr. Salazar will be ready to see you in a minute," one of the armed men told them. "If there's anything y'all need, just let me know," he said, looking only at Sonya, showing her that he was into her.

Almost ten minutes had passed before a man walked through a door on the opposite side of the room from the one they used to enter the waiting area. The office which they walked into looked and felt like power.

"Jay, it's good to see you. I'm sorry it's not on better terms."

"Mr. Salazar, I really don't know what this is about. I went over the books and they seem to be on point. If it's about the case them people are trying to put on me, well, trust me! I got my legal team on top of it."

"Well, that's pretty much the reason I called all of you here tonight."

Mr. Salazar turned and gave a signal to one of the seven armed men in the large office, and then the man walked out of the room through another door in the back of the office.

"You have an issue with rats that I can't sit back and wait for you to take care of on your own. It's not that I don't think you're able to deal with it. I'm just a lot better."

The man re-entered the room followed by Buckwild, Gully, and me.

"Oh, I see you are on top of it, but with all due respect, Salazar, I was holding off on things with them for a reason," J. Ross lied. "He just ain't been able to get up with us!"

"Jay, we've been going strong for too long for ya to think that me and my nigga had something to do with that shit that went down the last time ya seen us," I spoke up.

"I admit that I could've jumped the gun. Gully, I got a call from yo' fam explaining it all to me. Your pops was well respected, so I gave your uncle my word that I would give y'all a chance to clear y'all's names."

"Jay, I don't think that will be necessary unless you want to doubt my word?"

"No! If you say they're good, then that's all I need to hear. I hope this misunderstanding can be put behind us and we can get back to the money. To show my apologies, I'ma knock off a rack, and we're even on that bread y'all owe. Is we good?"

"Yeah, we good. But yo' fat-ass guy killed my bitch on some snake shit, and I'm not gonna hoe up on that there," Gully informed, wishing he still had his gun that the armed men had all of them give up on arrival to the warehouse.

J. Ross turned to Big Ed and asked, "What's he talkin' about? What you ain't been tellin' me?"

"I was gonna tell you about that shit, but it didn't go down like what he's talking about, and I don't know shit about a bitch getting killed. But we can handle it however the nigga wants."

"Now it's funny that ya say it didn't go down the way he said. I think Jay should be the judge."

Salazar looked at Gully and told him to tell J. Ross how it went down.

"Gully, can you please start from the beginning. That's my favorite part."

Gully told them about the night Alima was killed in Big Ed's drive-by in the parking lot of the downtown sports bar.

"Wait! What did you say your girl's name was again?" Sonya asked, after getting a text on her phone.

"Alima. Why, ya know her?"

"She's my cousin. I just got a text about her right now."

She handed the phone to J. Ross before turning on Big Ed and raining blows onto his face, obviously catching him off guard.

"Whoa! Whoa! Somebody get her off him before she kills him."

One of the men quickly ran to subdue Sonya. She had put it on his ass and had Big Ed knotted up and bloody that fast.

"Now go get our witness."

"Bitch, I'ma kill you for this!" Big Ed threatened Sonya.

"Fuck you, fat bitch! I would've killed yo' punk ass if it wasn't for Jay. But there ain't shit nobody can do to save ya from me when we leave this bitch. I promise you that!" she screamed at him.

"So you running around making moves in the dark, huh, fam?" J. Ross asked. "And yo' dumb ass leaving witnesses on some hot shit!"

"Jay, man, ain't no muthafucka see me. Just you wait 'til this so-called witness gets out here. The muthafucka don't know me, and if he do, I'ma kill him here on the spot. On everything, fam!"

"I'm glad you said that, because Gully didn't make it clear who you were there talking to."

"Oh, my bad. His rat ass was talkin' to a detective. I seen him handing him some papers and shit."

Gully didn't tell them that the papers he saw Big Ed give to the cop were actually cash.

Before Big Ed could get his lie out, two men dragged the badly beaten Detective Dickerson into the room.

"Jay, this is the officer he is talking about. As you can see, he admitted to everything with a little help."

"Hey, I don't know what this son of a bitch told y'all, but I was paying to make a charge go away on one of the folks."

"Stop it right there, you piece of shit. Now you taking me for a fool. Take him over there beside his friend and give Jay something to fix this shit with!" Salazar instructed his men.

They took hold of Big Ed, who didn't put up a fight with two guns pointed at his head. Another man rolled out some plastic and then pushed both him and the detective into it. The same man then handed J. Ross a gun.

"I'm not going to do this to you, Ed. My heart hurts that it's you. No, I'm not gonna do this shit," J. Ross said as he turned to Gully. "Here, my nigga, avenge yo' bitch."

"Say no mo'."

Gully walked over and took the gun outta J. Ross's hand and shot Big Ed twice in the body to hurt him but not kill him.

He then turned to Sonya.

"Come get some, ma. I'm not gonna do ya like that. If someone killed mine's, I'd want my part. I want you to know that I didn't want to leave her in the streets alone, but—!"

"No, you don't gotta explain. I ain't no lame bitch. I know you had to move around."

She accepted the gun from Gully.

"There's so much shit I wanna do to you right now, but this is what I want most."

She pulled the trigga and erased his face.

"Sonya, since you're already over there, would you take care of the rest of our rat problem, please. Thank you," J. Ross said to her.

She turned back around and quickly put two shots into Dickerson, instantly killing him on the spot.

"Now that you've got your house back in order, I want you to meet your new partner," Salazar announced as he turned to Buck and introduced him to J. Ross.

THIRTY-TWO

GP

I don't know why, but I agreed to hear Candi's side of the story. And if I didn't believe it, I promise you I was gonna kill that bitch right on the spot. Why did she have to be the one to save Apple? I told Apple to have Candi meet us over at my place, and then I told everyone else to be there as well.

"I'ma kill that punk bitch, GP. She's the reason I'm in this fuckin' chair!" Roc said as soon as he and Lyte got in the door.

"Chill, bro, she might not be the cause. I promised Apple we would hear Candi out."

"Fuck! I need something to smoke!" he said, before he then wheeled himself over to the table where my tray of kush was and got to rolling up a blunt.

The next knock at the door was Candi and her guy.

"Who ya got with you, Candi? It would've been nice to know ahead of time that a stranger was going to be comin' to my house."

"That's my bad, GP. She told me he was coming with her, and I just forgot to tell you," Apple admitted.

"Where is Wonda?" Candi asked while looking around the

room. "Oh my God, Roc! What happened to you?" she asked, seeing him in his wheelchair for the first time.

"Candi, don't say shit to me right now!"

"I didn't tell you about him because I didn't want to scare ya off from coming. But that's from that night Cal was killed," Apple explained to Candi.

"Ma, is yo' ass sure you wanna be here? Because it's not lookin' too friendly to me?" Vudu asked.

"What's yo' name, homie?" I asked, and he told me. "Okay! Well if I said she good, then that's what it is, especially up in my shit."

"Well, let's get this show on the road. I got places to be," he said, shifting his weight back and forth.

~ ~ ~

"Let me do this last song, and then we can be out, okay?"

"Go 'head. I just texted them and told them we will be there in a few minutes. If you wanna stay, I can just go by myself and come back when I'm done?"

"Nope! I want you to hear this song and tell me what ya think I should do with it. Plus, I got plans for that ass later, ma," Gully answered from inside the recording booth.

"Okay, let me hear it."

The engineer announced the track and then dropped the beat. Juicy sat next to him at the controls watching Gully get in his zone to do a song for her.

I know my future

Ma, I know our future

I know what you got and ya should put it on me

Girl don't try to hide it

Gone and put it on me

Put that in the pot and watch it millie jerk

Flip it, flip it

Til I pass up a thousand grams

Mr. Peter Pan with that butter man

Make all of my smokers hit the running man

That was way before I ever seen two hundred grand

Now I'm on a jet gettin' hella mileage

Land hop off in a limo

Tell the bitches pile in

Weed lit

I'm higher than a fuckin' pilot

Eyes closed

Dollar signs on the back of my eyelids

ALL WORK, NO PLAY

I told y'all before

I don't tell lies

I'm confident

I'm cocky

Ya can tell why

Ya heard I'm fallin' off

Now that's a damn lie

Seen more than they seen in they damn life

Mr. One Nighter

I never wife her

Her best friend around I'ma dike her

Been about this shit

Since I was in a diaper

Now I'm shittin' on the game

I den switched my life up

Up in the clouds and that's every day

Thinking how to be a billionaire

Like Bill Gates

Thinking how I could fuck that off in just one day

Yeah I can see the future

~ ~ ~

As soon as Gully walked in, he pulled his gun after recognizing Vudu from the alley.

"Whoa, my nigga! This ain't the place for whatever y'all got going on," Roc said, rolling between them.

"Gully, what's going on?" Juicy asked. "How ya gonna do this, my nigga?"

"Look, fam, I was doing my job; and as ya know, that job is over. I hope we can put this behind us, or just let us leave, and it's always another day?" Vudu proposed.

"Yeah, I'm thinkin' ya should leave 'cause I'm feelin' some type of way—bi-polar like. So what I say now may not mean shit in the next second," Gully told him and then stepped out of the way of the door.

Vudu shielded himself with Candi as he backed out, and the dumb bitch didn't even notice. All this shit was fucked up 'cause I still didn't get my answers. But like the nigga Gully said, there was always another day.

The End.

Text Good2Go at 31996 to receive new release updates via text message.

To order books, please fill out the order form below:
To order films please go to www.good2gofilms.com
Name: __ _____
Address:_____
City: _____ State: _____ Zip Code: _____
Phone:_____
Email: _____
Method of Payment: Check   VISA   MASTERCARD
Credit Card#:_ _____
Name as it appears on card: _____
Signature: _____

Item Name	Price	Qty	Amount
48 Hours to Die – Silk White	$14.99		
A Hustler's Dream - Ernest Morris	$14.99		
A Hustler's Dream 2 - Ernest Morris	$14.99		
A Thug's Devotion – J. L. Rose and J. M. McMillon	$14.99		
Black Reign – Ernest Morris	$14.99		
Bloody Mayhem Down South – Trayvon Jackson	$14.99		
Bloody Mayhem Down South 2 – Trayvon Jackson	$14.99		
Business Is Business – Silk White	$14.99		
Business Is Business 2 – Silk White	$14.99		
Business Is Business 3 – Silk White	$14.99		
Childhood Sweethearts – Jacob Spears	$14.99		
Childhood Sweethearts 2 – Jacob Spears	$14.99		
Childhood Sweethearts 3 - Jacob Spears	$14.99		
Childhood Sweethearts 4 - Jacob Spears	$14.99		
Connected To The Plug – Dwan Marquis Williams	$14.99		
Connected To The Plug 2 – Dwan Marquis Williams	$14.99		
Connected To The Plug 3 – Dwan Williams	$14.99		
Deadly Reunion – Ernest Morris	$14.99		
Dream's Life – Assa Raymond Baker	$14.99		
Flipping Numbers – Ernest Morris	$14.99		
Flipping Numbers 2 – Ernest Morris	$14.99		
He Loves Me, He Loves You Not - Mychea	$14.99		
He Loves Me, He Loves You Not 2 - Mychea	$14.99		
He Loves Me, He Loves You Not 3 - Mychea	$14.99		
He Loves Me, He Loves You Not 4 – Mychea	$14.99		

He Loves Me, He Loves You Not 5 – Mychea	$14.99		
Lord of My Land – Jay Morrison	$14.99		
Lost and Turned Out – Ernest Morris	$14.99		
Married To Da Streets – Silk White	$14.99		
M.E.R.C. - Make Every Rep Count Health and Fitness	$14.99		
Money Make Me Cum – Ernest Morris	$14.99		
My Besties – Asia Hill	$14.99		
My Besties 2 – Asia Hill	$14.99		
My Besties 3 – Asia Hill	$14.99		
My Besties 4 – Asia Hill	$14.99		
My Boyfriend's Wife - Mychea	$14.99		
My Boyfriend's Wife 2 – Mychea	$14.99		
My Brothers Envy – J. L. Rose	$14.99		
My Brothers Envy 2 – J. L. Rose	$14.99		
Naughty Housewives – Ernest Morris	$14.99		
Naughty Housewives 2 – Ernest Morris	$14.99		
Naughty Housewives 3 – Ernest Morris	$14.99		
Naughty Housewives 4 – Ernest Morris	$14.99		
Never Be The Same – Silk White	$14.99		
Shades of Revenge – Assa Raymond Baker	$14.99		
Slumped – Jason Brent	$14.99		
Someone's Gonna Get It – Mychea	$14.99		
Stranded – Silk White	$14.99		
Supreme & Justice – Ernest Morris	$14.99		
Supreme & Justice 2 – Ernest Morris	$14.99		
Supreme & Justice 3 – Ernest Morris	$14.99		
Tears of a Hustler - Silk White	$14.99		
Tears of a Hustler 2 - Silk White	$14.99		
Tears of a Hustler 3 - Silk White	$14.99		
Tears of a Hustler 4- Silk White	$14.99		
Tears of a Hustler 5 – Silk White	$14.99		
Tears of a Hustler 6 – Silk White	$14.99		
The Panty Ripper - Reality Way	$14.99		
The Panty Ripper 3 – Reality Way	$14.99		

The Solution – Jay Morrison	$14.99		
The Teflon Queen – Silk White	$14.99		
The Teflon Queen 2 – Silk White	$14.99		
The Teflon Queen 3 – Silk White	$14.99		
The Teflon Queen 4 – Silk White	$14.99		
The Teflon Queen 5 – Silk White	$14.99		
The Teflon Queen 6 - Silk White	$14.99		
The Vacation – Silk White	$14.99		
Tied To A Boss - J.L. Rose	$14.99		
Tied To A Boss 2 - J.L. Rose	$14.99		
Tied To A Boss 3 - J.L. Rose	$14.99		
Tied To A Boss 4 - J.L. Rose	$14.99		
Tied To A Boss 5 - J.L. Rose	$14.99		
Time Is Money - Silk White	$14.99		
Tomorrow's Not Promised – Robert Torres	$14.99		
Tomorrow's Not Promised 2 – Robert Torres	$14.99		
Two Mask One Heart – Jacob Spears and Trayvon Jackson	$14.99		
Two Mask One Heart 2 – Jacob Spears and Trayvon Jackson	$14.99		
Two Mask One Heart 3 – Jacob Spears and Trayvon Jackson	$14.99		
Wrong Place Wrong Time – Silk White	$14.99		
Young Goonz – Reality Way	$14.99		
Subtotal:			
Tax:			
Shipping (Free) U.S. Media Mail:			
Total:			

Make Checks Payable To:
Good2Go Publishing
7311 W Glass Lane,
Laveen, AZ 85339